KIKI SWINSON

CHEAPER to KEEP HER

THE HUNT IS ON

PART **6**

A NOVEL

NIQUE

Publisher's address:
K.S. Publications
P.O. Box 68878
Virginia Beach, VA 23471

Website: **www.KikiMedia.net**
Email: **KS.publications@yahoo.com**
Instagram.com/**AllthingsKikiSwinson**
Twitter.com/**AuthorKikiSwinson**
Facebook.com/**KikiSwinson**

ISBN-13: 978-0986203770
ISBN-10: 0986203777

First Edition: October 2019
10 9 8 7 6 5 4 3 2 1
Editors: Letitia Carrington
Interior & Cover Design: Marion Designs
Cover Photo: Marion Designs

Printed in the United States of America

Don't Miss Out On These Other Titles:

Don't Miss Out On These Other Titles Cont.—

CHEAPER to KEEP HER

THE HUNT IS ON

PART **6**

A NOVEL
UNIQUE

KS Publications
www.KikiMedia.net

CHAPTER ONE

Lynise

I lied there in the hospital bed with consumed with fear because the only person I trusted was now fighting for his own life. What's going to happen to me if he doesn't survive? How am I going to live my life? Who's going to protect me? I can't think of anyone right now that will give me the level of mental and physical security that Agent Sean Foster gave me. During the next hour, my bed was rolled onto a nearby elevator and then onto another floor. After I was placed in a new room, two nurses, a doctor, and two uniformed police officers paraded and then out of my room. I knew why the doctor and the nurses were in here, but the sight of the police officers crowding my space gave me a level of anxiety that I couldn't ignore. "Do you really have to be here?" I asked a black cop after the doctor, and one of the nurses left. He was standing by the door with his arms folded like he was ready to take on anyone that made a sudden move.

"Yes, ma'am, I'm afraid we have to." He replied.

"Well, could you wait on the outside of my door? Because I could really use some privacy right now." I told him.

"I'm sorry, but I'm afraid not." He said apologetically.

"And why not? I don't want to lay here and see your face all day long. I want to be in my room alone. So, whoever you need to run this by, I need to see them now." I said, my level of anger began to rise. The white nurse that was left inside the room with me saw that I was getting upset and interjected. "Officer, I know you're supposed to secure this area, but when you're interfering with the well-being of the patient, we have to intervene." The nurse told him.

"Nurse, I understand what you're saying, but I was ordered not to leave this room. So, you're gonna have to take this up with my commanding officer." He explained.

"Well, where is your commanding officer? I wanna speak to him." I roared.

The monitor hooked up to me that read my vital signs started chirping at an alarming rate. The nurse turned towards me and started pressing buttons on the monitor device that was reading off my vital signs. "Sir, please leave the room." The nurse said abruptly while trying to minimize the noise the machine was giving off. Without saying another word, the cop left my room and closed the door behind himself. Once the nurse and I were in the room alone, I let out a long sigh. "Thank you for that," I said.

"Don't mention it," she started off, "He was a serious dick head if you ask me." She continued as she stuffed the bloody sheets that were on my bed into a hazardous, plastic bin by the door. The sight of the sheets sickened me on the inside. I needed to know what was going on with Agent Sean. "Could you please find out where he is and see if he's all right?" I asked her, sitting straight up in the bed.

"They have him in surgery right now. So, I won't know his condition until after they're done with him." She explained.

"I heard the cops saying that he was shot while trying to protect me. Is that true? Was he really shielding my body with his to keep those guys from shooting me?" I wanted to know.

"Yes, that's what I heard. He's a courageous man." She commented.

Instantly tears filled my eyes until they could no longer hold, and then the flood gates opened. Picturing Agent Sean covering my body with his so that I wouldn't get shot melted my heart. I mean, who'd do that for someone? Nobody I know; except Agent Sean Foster. "How many times did he get shot?" I continued to question her.

"I'm not sure. But I know it was a lot."

Fully crying now, I sat in the bed helplessly. "God, please let 'em live. Spare his life. He's a good guy, with a good heart." I began to cry out loud.

The nurse stood next to my bed and began to rub my back in a circular motion. "You keep praying, and I'm sure God will see him through this it." She said in a comforting way. But it didn't help me feel any better about this situation. Agent Sean was in surgery fighting for his life, and I'm lying here in this bed, and I can't do anything for him. If he weren't protecting me from that gun battle from earlier, I'd be in surgery, and he'd be okay.

While I wallowed in my sorrow, the nurse handed me a box of tissue paper, and then she checked my vitals and made sure my wires were connected properly. "I'm gonna give you some time for yourself. But if you need anything, push the red call button next to the power button of that TV remote." She instructed me.

I responded by nodding my head while wiping the tears away from my face. Immediately after the nurse left the room, I laid my head back on the pillow and balled my eyes out. Tears were running down my face at a rapid pace. "Father God, please don't let him die. I don't know what I'll do without him. He didn't deserve to be shot. So, I beg you to bring him out of this Lord God! Please, I will do anything. I promise I will go to church and give my life to you totally," I prayed sincerely as I could because I knew it was out of my hands. Only God had the power to turn this situation around for Agent Sean.

Not too long after the nurse left, I heard a knock on the door. "Who is it?" I asked while still wiping the tears from my eyes and face. The door opened, and in comes the same nurse. As soon as our eyes met, she gave me a look of despair, and I knew right then that Agent Sean was either in worse shape or that he was dead. My heart sunk into the pit of my stomach. "Please don't tell me that he's dead," I told her.

She stood at the door and gave me a head nod. I tried to jump out of my bed, but she rushed towards me and stopped me in my tracks. "No, get off me! I've gotta see him." I shouted.

"I'm sorry, but I can't let you do that." She told me, trying to prevent me from getting out of bed.

"But I need to see him. I love him. He's my lifeline." I cried out. I wanted to see Agent Sean Foster, and I felt that if the entire hospital heard my pain, then someone would let me see him. Unfortunately, that didn't happen. The nurse alerted other nurses to come to my room by pressing a button from her pager that was fastened on the pocket of her scrubs. Within seconds, two nurses and two uniformed police officers rushed in.

"What's the problem?" One of the officers asked the nurse.

"She's trying to get out of bed, so I need you guys to help me scrap her down." She told them.

"No, don't strap me down. All I wanna do is see Agent Sean." I shouted. And then I started screaming at the top of my lungs. "Get away from me! Don't touch me!"

My words fell on death ears. It took both cops and the hospital staff to pin me down and strap me to my bed. And before I knew it, one of the nurses put something in my IV that made me calm down and eventually caused me to feel somewhat tired. Whatever it was didn't send me to sleep, but I was close. In fact, everything around me seemed like it was going in slow motion. I'm talking movement and verbal exchanges between the cops and the hospital staff. I tried talking too, but it felt like it was taking forever for me to communicate my feelings, so I laid there and watched what was going on around me.

****

I can't tell you how long I was faded, but I can tell you that as soon as that drug wore off me, I was right back where I started; asking a bunch of questions and was waiting to be answered. There was a different nurse in the room with me when I regained my faculties. So, that told me that the hospital shift changed. I also noticed that I was still strapped to the bed and I didn't like this one bit. "Why am I strapped to this bed? Take this shit off me now!" I said in an irritated manner.

"I'm sorry, I don't have the authority to do that." The nurse told me.

I got a little more irritated. "Well, who has the authority? I need to see them now."

"Your doctor," The nurse replied while typing on the computer keys in front of the monitor on wheels.

"Would you call him in here?" I wanted to know.

"He's on another floor right now."

"Well is there someone else I could talk to? I don't like being restricted like this. Y'all are treating me like I'm a psych patient."

"Well, those are not his intentions." She continued typing, only looking back at me once more.

"Where are the cops? Are they still here?" I wondered aloud.

"Yes, there's two of them outside the door. Do you want me to get 'em?"

"No. I don't wanna see 'em." I said, and then I paused for a moment. "What are you typing?"

"I'm just updating your vitals and the meds that have been given to you."

"While I watched her document my information into the computer, I immediately started thinking about Agent Sean Foster. And then it hit me that the last time his name was mentioned was when someone said that he died. Was this true? Or was I dreaming? No way. This can't be true. I knew I had to be dreaming. But I needed to be sure. "Did Agent Sean Foster really die in surgery?" the question filtered from my mouth.

She turned around and looked me straight in my eyes and said, "Yes, I'm afraid so."

Once more, my heartfelt like a dagger went through it. Instantly filled with pain and anguish, my heart collapsed into the pit of my stomach. "No, please don't tell me that. I know him. He's a strong man. He can pull through anything." I pointed out.

"I am so sorry for your loss. I heard he was a good man. A brave one too. They said that he saved your life." She explained.

Tears poured from my eyes uncontrollably as I laid there strapped to the bed, trying to come to terms with Agent Sean really being dead. He was my protector. My lover. He understood me and knew what I needed. So, who's going to look after me now? There was literally no one that could be trusted. His agent colleagues didn't like me, nor did the local police. They all hated the ground I walked on. So, where do I go from here? Who do I turn to?

Somewhat feeling my pain, the nurse handed me a handful of tissue paper to wipe my eyes. "I know it may not seem like it now, but you will get past this." She said. I knew she was trying to encourage me, but I couldn't receive it. I was all alone. I didn't have one single person in my fucking corner. Absolutely no one. Not one soul.

Instead of commenting, I laid there and reminisced all the good times I shared with him. The times that he and I made love to each other stood out in my mind. He loved me hard, and he made sure that I knew it. I'd never had a man to treat me the way he did. Agent Sean was a real man in my book, and I wasn't afraid to let the world know it.

Consumed in deep though, didn't prepare me for what was next. "Coming in," I heard a male voice announced. Startled, I looked in the direction of the door. Standing there, dressed in plain clothes was a Caucasian woman. She got the nurse's attention too.

"Can I help you?" she asked the woman.

She flashed her badge and told us who she was, "My name is Special Agent Helen Hunt. And I am here to speak with Lynise," she declared.

"So, you're the new agent that's supposed to watch my back?"

"As a matter of fact, I am," she replied and then she started walking towards my bed. "Could I have a few minutes with her alone?" The agent said to the nurse.

"Sure, I can do that." She replied and then she stepped away from the computer and exited the room.

"Why do they have you strapped to the bed?" She wanted to know.

"I don't know. I told the nurse to get someone in here so they could take this shit off me." I didn't mince words.

Agent Hunt took a seat in the chair next to my bed. "It looks uncomfortable, so I'll speak with someone before I leave." She assured me.

"I would appreciate it." I thanked her. "So, are you going to tell me why you're here?" I got to the point.

"I'm here because I'm acting as the new supervisor on this detail since we loss Agent Foster."

Without warning, I started balling my eyes out. To hear the words that we lost, Agent Sean felt like a dagger plunged through my heart. "Please don't say that," I sobbed. "It's not true," I told her.

She plaid her right hand on my leg. "I know that this is hard, and you don't want to believe it, but it's true."

"If everybody is saying that he's dead, can I go and see it for myself?"

"I'm afraid I can't allow that to happen. It's against

9

hospital policy, and he's the property of the federal government."

"So, that's it? I can't speak to someone else about this?"

"I'm afraid not." She said firmly.

"That's bullshit!" I snapped. My cries turned from sobbing to rage.

Agent Hunt gave me a hard stare. "Am I missing something?" She asked me.

"Missing something???? What are you talking about?" I wondered aloud. I needed clarity.

"Is it true about you and Agent Foster? Did you two have an affair?"

"Yes, we were. He was my lover." I said boldly. I would've screamed it to the mountain tops if I could've. But I was strapped down to a hospital bed in a room no bigger than a jail cell. "How long was this affair going on?" Her questions continued.

"Not too long after I was put into witness protection."

"So, you two were intimate?"

"If you wanna know if we were fucking each other, then yes we were. He was my man." I let her know.

"You do know that that wasn't supposed to happen? If my bosses and I had known this was going on when Agent Foster was alive, he would've been pulled off this detail and possibly fired from the bureau."

"Well, as you can see, it's too late for that. He's fucking gone now. And it's all because he loved me to the point that he wasn't going to let those savages run into the hospital and kill me. Every bullet he took was a bullet that was meant for me." I continued sobbing.

"Who else knew about your affair with Agent Foster?"

"Everybody that was in the safe house knew about it. It wasn't a secret. Even that female agent knew about us. The way she was acting around me made me think that they had a relationship once upon a time. And where is she anyway? I betcha she got a chance to see Sean's body." I said, gritting my teeth.

"Agent Zachary is dead. Her body was found in the trunk of her rental car about an hour ago."

"Well, I guess she'll be able to see Agent Sean in the afterlife," I said nonchalantly. But I was angrier than anything. It's like that bitch gets the edge over me all the time.

"Maybe she does, who knows. What we need to be more concerned about is keeping you safe until we're able to move you back into a safe house."

"You mean to tell me that I've got to go back into witness protection?"

"Yes, you do. Because remember Bishop is still alive. And until we have him behind bars and everyone's testimonies that would put him away for life, we have to move with caution."

"When am I getting out of here?" I blurted out. I figured why not ask since I'm still in their custody.

"In a couple of days. But I've gotta keep it under wraps to prevent what happened earlier from happening again."

"Are you guys gonna have agents standing outside

my room? 'Cause right now; there are uniform cops hanging outside. There was even one guarding my room from in here. He was standing against the wall right behind you. And when I told the jerk off to get out, he told me that he didn't have to. The nurse that was in here when you walked in finally told him to get lost, so he did."

"Before I leave the hospital, I will talk to the head housing administrator and see if we can get these straps off you."

"Thank you. I really appreciate you doing that for me. Because when I asked the nurse to take these restraints off me, she told me that she didn't have the authority to do so."

"She doesn't. But I will take care of it."

Before I could thank her again, my room door opened and in came a black male in a doctor's coat. I assumed that he was the doctor, so I spoke up first. "Are you my doctor?"

"No, I'm the physician's assistant. But we do almost the same things." He replied as he closed the door behind himself.

"We need to get these restraints taken off her." Agent Hunt spoke up.

"Sure, I can arrange that. But she's gonna have to promise my staff and me that she's going to be on her best behavior from this day forward." He said nicely.

Agent Hunt looked back at me. "You're not gonna give his staff any more problems, right?" she asked me in front of him.

I sighed heavily and said, "Yes, I won't give anyone else any problems."

"Okay great. I will have nurse Betty come in here and remove your restraints but other than that, how are you feeling? I saw the photos of you after that car accident you were in, and you were pretty banged up. Not to mention, what happened earlier when those guys shot up your other hospital room. You've got to be shaking up by that." He said like he was probing me for answers.

"I don't remember any of that. I didn't wake up until after they carried Agent Foster out of my room."

"Do you feel any soreness in your arms or legs? Maybe your back?" He continued to probe me.

"Now that I think about it, I feel a little bit of pain in my neck and my left arm."

"Well, we'll give you something for that. But for now, just take it easy." He advised me.

"Do you know when she could be released?" Agent Hunt interjected.

"To be on the safe side, I could see releasing her in the next two to three days. No sooner than that, though."

"Okay, great." Agent Hunt said.

The physician's assistant hung out in the room for only a couple of minutes. After he listened to my heartbeat and checked my vitals, he reassured me that he was going to have the nurse come in to release me from the straps within the hour and that I was going to make a speedy recovery if I followed his instructions in and out of the hospital. I told him that I would.

Not too long after the physician left my room, Agent

13

hunt wrapped up our conversation by telling me that she'd be coming by to see me the following day and then she reminded me not to give the hospital staff any more trouble. "They're gonna take off the restraints, so don't give them a reason to put them back on." She warned me.

"Tell them to stay out of my room," I demanded.

"Who are you talking about? The doctors. The nurses?"

"No, those fake ass cops standing outside my door."

"Oh, you don't have to worry about them. As soon as one of my agents get here, he will relieve those guys in the hallway, and you won't have to worry about them anymore. But other than that, do you have any questions for me?" She asked me after she stood up from the chair.

I hesitated for a moment, trying to jog my memory and search my mind to see if I had anything pressing that I needed her to weigh in on, but my mind went blank. My heart was troubled, but I didn't have the words to express them. Agent Hunt stood there with a puzzled look on her face. "What's on your mind?"

"That's the thing... I don't know." I said with confusion.

She reached inside her jacket pocket and pulled a business card from it. She placed it in the center of my right hand, and then she folded my hand into a fold. "Call me if you have any more problems, or at the least want to talk."

I gave her a head nod.

****

After Agent Hunt exited my room, I couldn't help but wonder why she was so nice to me? All the other agents working on my detail alongside Agent Sean hated my freaking guts. So, was she being genuine, or was this all a front? I do know one thing, and that is, she frowned upon my relationship with Agent Sean. There was no denying that that gave her a bad taste in her mouth. But at this point, talking about how he would've been taken off my detail and or fired was a day late and a dollar short. He's gone now, and he's not coming back.

Wallowing in sorrows about losing Agent Sean was consuming me. Every time I saw his face in my head, my heart gets heavier and heavier. And before I knew it, I was sobbing all over again. "God, why him?" I began to pray aloud. "Why did you take him from me, Father God? Sean was a good man. He was making a difference in the world, and he loved me. So, again, why him?" I mourned.

Visions of Agent Sean and I talking and laughing while eating was one of those moments when I felt the love from him. He was the ideal man for me regardless of what Agent Hunt and the other agents say. I guess now; I won't be with him again until cross over into the next life. And if Agent Zachary is running down on his heels, then I'm going to stop her right in her tracks. Agent Sean is my soulmate. Nothing more…. Nothing less.

The next knock on my door came about twenty minutes later. That person announced themselves before pushing the door open. "It's Nurse Betty," she said.

"You can come in," I told her.

Seconds later, she pushed the door open and entered my room with a smile. "Just got word to take off your restraints." She told me as she walked pulled a pair of blue, latex gloves from the box next to the door.

I sighed. "Boy, am I glad to hear that."

"I was too when I got the order from my supervisor." She continued as she walked towards me.

I started sniffling and trying to hold back what tears I had left, so my vision could be clear while I watched the nurse relieve me from these straps.

"I'm gonna give you some tissue paper to wipe your eyes and face once I free your hands." She offered.

"Thank you," I replied.

The straps that were binding me to the bed were thick cotton straps that resembled the design of a straitjacket. The seal of Velcro was heavy duty and was impossible for me to get out of it on my own. Now it only took a minute and a half for Nurse Betty to take off the left arm restraint and less than that time for the second one. It felt like a weight had been lifted off me when she finally freed me. I sat the agent's business card down on my lap, and then I started massaging my wrists.

"Feel better?" She asked me.

"Much better." I declared.

"Well, don't give them another reason to put them back on." She warned me.

"I won't," I assured her and then I changed the subject. "Do think that I could get a little exercise by taking a walk on the floor.

"For your safety, I don't think that will happen. But you're more than welcome to ask one of the officers standing outside your door."

I frowned and rolled my eyes after hearing Nurse Betty's response. She saw my mood change and said, "Don't you wanna be safe?"

"Of course, I do, but I don't wanna be cooped up in this room when I walk around. Nothing is restricting me from standing on my feet."

"That may be true, but your safety outweighs getting exercise on any scale." Nurse Betty wouldn't let up. "But I will ask the officers outside the door and see what they say," she continued and then she strolled out of my room.

I sat there in my bed and waited to hear Nurse Betty's voice and whomever she was going to speak with concerning me. I sat there for the first 10 seconds and heard nothing. Then another 10 seconds went by, and still, there was nothing. So, I got out of my bed and rushed over to the door. When I opened the door, no one was there. This completely caught me off guard. Anxiety consumed me at that very moment. I didn't know whether to close the door or make a run for it. My mind was spinning out of control. "Come on, Lynise, you can do it. Make a run for it." I gave myself a pep talk. "Do it for Agent Sean." I urged myself. With every ounce of willpower, I had inside of me; I finally made up my mind to make a run for it. So, when I peered around the doorway and saw that Nurse Betty was standing a few feet away speaking quietly to an informed police officer, my hopes of leaving my room vanished into thin air. I wanted to yell and get their attention, but then I decided against it. I didn't want to bring any attention to myself, so I stepped back away from the door, and then I closed it as quietly as I could to prevent them from hearing it.

Instead of getting right back in the bed, I went inside the bathroom to pee. While I was on the toilet, I heard a knock on my room door. "I'm in the bathroom," I yelled, hoping that I was being listened to.

"It's Nurse Betty," I heard her reply outside my bathroom door.

"Did you talk to someone?" I asked her, even though I knew the answer.

"Yes, Officer Knox said that he couldn't make that call because he was told by his supervisor that you are not allowed to leave out of your room."

"And how long is that gonna be? They are treating me like a caged bird." I protested. By this time, I had stood up from the toilet, flushed it, and began to wash my hands.

"I'm assuming until the two federal agents that are assigned to you come here and relieve him." Nurse Betty explained.

I let out a long sigh. "Alright," I said.

Nurse Betty had her back turned and was leaving the room by the time I was entirely out of the bathroom. I walked back over to my bed and climbed on top of it. After I pulled the covers over me and turned on my side with my back facing the door, I grabbed the remote and started sifting through the channels. I couldn't believe that I couldn't find anything good to watch. But then I realized that it wasn't the programs on TV, it was me. I couldn't get Agent Sean's face out of my head. And before I realized it, I was filled up with sorrow and then I broke down into tears.

Thinking about the first day, I met him and the many times he took my side when the other agents were giving me flack. He stood up for me every time he felt like they were annoying me, and that spoke volumes to me. I've never in my life had a man to have my back the way Agent Sean Foster did. He was a real nigga in my eyes. And no other man, in my opinion, would ever be able to hold a candle to him. That's some real shit!

My whole journey up until now has been one roller coaster ride. It seems like it was yesterday when I started working as a bartender at the strip club. From there, I met Duke Carrington's evil ass. And after he used me up, he kicked me and my clothes out of his condo in the Cosmopolitan Building. Then Bishop steps up to the plate. He had me thinking that he was my guardian angel. My night and shining armor. But he was a piece of fucking shit like Duke Carrington was. The difference between the two is, Duke is death, and Bishop wasn't. Which brings me to this, Bishop needs to meet his maker before he causes me to meet mine.

CHAPTER TWO
Whitney

It was pretty hard for my mother and me to drive down south to see my brother Sean's body. Sean was my twin brother, born three minutes before I did so he always boasted about being the older sibling. Growing up with him was an adventure. He did everything together from playing hide and seek to skateboarding up and down our block. We always had a solid bond. After we graduated from high school, he went off to Penn State and received a Master's Degree in law, while I attended Howard University and received a Bachelor's Degree in Pediatric and Child Health. My goal was to get my master's degree, but my father fell ill and five months later passed away, so I took some time off from school so I could help my mother cope with the loss. Sean only took one week of leave because he had just been recruited by the FBI. No one held it against him, but Sean always carried that guilt around with him.

After one year of my father's passing, I convinced my

boyfriend Jeff to move in my parents' house with me because I knew my mother needed me and I took a position as an Assistant Director of Patient Services at a Pediatric Clinic. And now that we've lost my brother will further put a damper on me and my mother's life. I guess all we can do now is be there for one another.

When we arrived in Virginia, we met up with Special Agent Saunders, who was appointed to escort my mother and me to the county morgue to view Sean's body. He was a strait-laced Uncle Tom type of a guy, but on the flip side, he was very friendly and accommodating. Every word was yes ma'am, no ma'am. He held open every door we walked through, and he took the lead at the appropriate times. While my mom was shading tears over the fact that we lost Sean and the condition of his body, Agent Saunders even offered several words of condolences and mentioned that if we needed anything that he could take care of it personally.

On our way out of the morgue, my mother asked Agent Saunders if we could see the woman that Sean sacrificed his life for. He quickly shot the idea down, but my mother wasn't taking no for an answer. It took her about five minutes to change his mind, but in the end, she won.

The ride on the elevator felt like an eternity. The walk to this woman's room took even longer. And during this walk, I watched my mother as she walked with her head high, looking like she was about to conquer the world. But I knew what she wanted. She needed closure, and I suppose this woman that my brother risked his life for had the answer for her.

As approached the door of her room, Agent Saunders flashed his badge to a black, male US Marshal who was sitting in a chair outside in the hallway. After he gave us the green light to enter, I took a death breath and exhaled because I had no idea how things were going to go once, we came face to face with the woman that my brother fought to keep alive.

"Are you ladies ready?" He asked my mother and me.

"As ready as we'll ever be," I replied.

My mother smiled while the agent knocked on the door. "Ms. Washington, you have guests." The agent announced from the hallway. "Are you dressed?" He continued.

"Who wants to know?" She yelled from the other side of the door. She seemed annoyed at the idea that my mother and I were there to see her. I wanted so badly to hurl obscenities through the door and tell her to fuck off. But this meeting was for my mother, not me. So, I left well enough alone.

"Agent Foster's family wants to meet you." He told her.

"Who?" She replied, sounding a little apprehensive.

"Can we come in?" He asked again.

"Yeah, you can come in," she finally said.

Agent Saunders pushed the door, opened slowly, and walked in the room. My mother followed him, and I followed her. The moment my eyes landed on this infamous woman, I caught while she was trying to sit straight up in the bed. I noticed a few scratches and bruises on and around her face. But those minor scrapes and scars were nothing like the bullet wounds that were inflicted on my brother's body. In my eyes, she made out like a bandit.

"Lynise, my name Special Agent Saunders," he introduced himself and shook her hands. As soon as he let her hand go, he pointed to my mother and me and said, "and this is Special Agent Foster's mother, Mrs. Ester Foster and his sister Whitney Foster."

"Nice to meet you Lynise," My mother smiled and shook her hand, but I gave her a head nod, and in turn, she gave me a head nod back and smiled.

"Nice to meet you too," she replied.

From where I was standing, I will admit that she was a cute girl. I can see why Sean was attracted to her. But there was something about her that didn't sit well with me. I can't quite put my finger on it now, but who knows, I may figure it out before I leave this room.

"How are you feeling?" My mother's questions started.

"I'm feeling better." She stated cautiously. I could tell that our presence was making her nervous. My mother sensed it too.

"We're not making you feel uncomfortable, are we?" My mother wanted to know.

"No... no.... I'm good. It's just that I'm surprised to see you." She responded.

"I was just as surprised when she asked to meet you," Agent Saunders chimed in.

"I second that..." I interjected. If it were up to me, I

would've walked out of the morgue, headed straight back to my car and would not have looked back.

"Please don't be mad at me for what happened to your son. I loved him so much! He was my world! Believe me; I probably loved him just as much as you two did," she said.

"You couldn't have possibly loved my brother as much as me, and my mother did. She carried him inside of her for nine months, and she raised him from birth. I'm his twin. We shared the same blood, and our bond was like no other." I replied sarcastically.

"I'm sorry, I didn't mean it like that. I was only trying to tell you how much he meant to me." She chimed back in.

"Well, be careful the next time," I warned her.

"Are you guys here to take him back to your hometown?" She changed the subject.

"The Federal Bureau is handling that for them." Agent Saunders interjected.

"Where will the funeral be?" She questioned us again.

"All of those arrangements will also be handled by the bureau." Agent Saunders announced.

"Think I can go?" She blurted out.

"I'm afraid that that's not gonna happen. The federal bureau has strict policies concerning an agent and a witness." Agent Saunders explained.

"That's bullshit, and you know it!" She protested.

"Now only is it against witness protection policy, it wouldn't be safe for you either." He continued.

"I don't care about that. I wanna see him before you guys put him in the ground." She snapped. I could tell that she was getting extremely irritated by Agent Saunders answers.

"Rules are rules. But I'll tell you what, maybe I could take a couple of photos of him and give them to you. Give you something to hold on to." Agent Saunders tried to compromise.

"I don't want any damn pictures. I wanna see him." She continued to protest, but Agent Saunders wasn't letting up. He stuck to his word, and when he realized that Lynise wasn't giving up the fight to see Sean, he grabbed his cell phone from his inside jacket pocket and excused himself from the room. "I have a call to make so I'll be outside when you ladies are done." He said as he walked away.

"How freaking convenient!!" She spat.

"You're a firecracker!" My mother commented.

"If you've been through what I've been through this past year, you will act the same way," Lynise said, justifying her actions.

"It's okay; I understand what you're trying to say. I remember when he first called me and told me that he finally found the love of his life." My mother began to explain, disregarding the fact that the FBI agent had just left the room.

"He did?" Lynise replied cheerfully. She was also unconcerned by the agent, leaving the room abruptly.

My mother smiled. "Yes. He also told me that you were a mess too."

Lynise found what my mother said funny, so she

chuckled. "Yeah, I gave him a pretty hard time when we first met. But when it was all said and done, he had the last word."

"Yep, that's Sean." My mother commented and smiled.

"Have you seen him yet?" Lynise asked, looking at us both.

"Yes, we saw him." My mother told her.

"How does he look? I've been trying to get them to let me go and see him, but no one will let me out of this room." She said.

"He looks like he's resting."

"No, he doesn't mom. Tell her the truth. Tell her how many bullets he took for her." I interjected. I was tired of all the smiling and hoopla going back and forth between them.

"Whitney, stop it! That's not necessary." My mother tried to silence me. But I wasn't going for it. My brother was dead, and it was all because of this bad luck ass federal witness that couldn't keep her legs closed.

"No mama, this is necessary. Sean is dead. And he's dead because he put his life on the line for this floozie!" I spat. My blood was boiling in my veins by this point.

"I am not a floozie for one. And so, you know, it kills me inside to know that he took those bullets for me. I told you that I loved your brother and as God as my witness if I could take his place, I would." She explained as her eyes became watery.

My mother rushed to her side and embraced her in her arms. "Come on, Whitney; it's really not her fault. Sean knew what he was doing when he signed up to be an FBI agent." My mother reasoned as she held Lynise in her arms.

"It's okay Mrs. Ester; I would feel the same way if I was in her shoes." Lynise sobbed.

Was this bitch trying to get my mother to feel sorry for her? If she was, then she was doing an excellent job of it. "Mom, why are you consoling her? I'm the one hurting behind Sean's murder." I questioned her.

Before my mother could answer me, we heard a knock at the door. "Coming in," a woman announced. Then a nurse appeared from behind the door. "Could you ladies clear the room for a minute? I need to talk to Lynise in private," she continued.

"No, it's okay. You can talk around them." Lynise told her.

The nurse looked at my mother and me, and then she looked at Lynise as if she wasn't sure if talking around us was a good idea. "It's okay." Lynise insisted while my mother stood by her bed.

The nurse took a deep breath, and then she exhaled. "While running a few tests with the blood samples we took from you, we found out that you're pregnant." The nurse finally said.

My mother gasped and turned her attention back to Lynise while Lynise sat in her bed with a surprised expression on her face. She was definitely at a loss for words. "Are you sure?" she asked the nurse.

"Yes, I'm sure. We ran three tests, and all three came back positive." The nurse assured her.

"Oh, my God! Are you carrying my grandbaby?" My

mother wanted to know. She stood there like she was a big ball of emotions. I didn't know if she wanted to kiss Lynise or hug her.

"He's the only man I've been with, so yes, I guess I am." She answered my mother.

After getting the answer she wanted, she leaned in and gave Lynise a huge hug. "Those evil men took away my son, but God repays me by giving me a grandbaby. Thank you, Jesus!" She celebrated, holding Lynise for dear life, it seemed.

I stood there with disgust on my face. This bitch doesn't need to be rewarded for carrying my brother's baby. She was the fucking reason that he got killed.

"Does the test say how far along I am?" Lynise asked the nurse.

The nurse smiled, "yes, you're eight weeks." She replied. "Oh, thank you, Jesus, for this miracle." My mother continued to celebrate this moment. The sight of them both made me upset, so I turned around and left the room. How could they celebrate when my twin brother just got murdered? I know one thing, I'm going to deal with my mother later on about this because she's losing sight of why we came to Virginia in the first place. Hopefully, things between us don't fall apart.

CHAPTER THREE

Lynise

I can't believe Whitney left the room, after finding out from the nurse that I was pregnant with Sean's baby. She should be happy that I'm giving her a niece or nephew. Mrs. Ester was overjoyed by the news. "Do you think Whitney's mad that I'm pregnant?" I asked Mrs. Ester.

"Oh, don't worry about her, she's gonna be fine," Mrs. Ester assured me.

"I never knew that Sean had a twin sister," I said.

"I'm surprised that he didn't tell you."

"We never talked about his personal life. Where was he born? How many siblings he had? He was a very guarded person."

"Well, you were always a topic of discussion when he called to check in with me."

"Really? What did he say?" I asked. I was very eager to

find out just how much he loved me. I gave Mrs. Ester my full attention.

"Well, he couldn't tell me much about you because he was assigned to protect you under the witness protection program. But he did tell me how beautiful you were and how smitten he was about you. He told me that if you weren't in the program, that he would've married you by now."

"Really? He said that?" I replied cheerfully. Hearing Sean's mother tell me that he loved me was the best feeling in the world. I knew that he loved me, but I didn't know that I meant that much to him that he'd tell his mother about it. I swear I feel like a star in the sky.

"Yes, he did." She said confidently.

"Wow! I don't know what to say," I began to say, and then I fell silent. My feelings were all over the place. I wanted to shout to the heavens and tell the world that I loved Sean with all my heart, but then I remembered where I was; the hospital with law enforcement as my protection and they wouldn't like it one bit. I thanked her instead and told her how much it meant for her to tell me that. She embraced me again and told me not to mention it. She and I talked for another a few more minutes; that is until Agent Saunders walked back into the room and interrupted us.

"I hate to break this up, but I've gotta head back to the office, and before I'm able to do that, I have to escort you ladies off this floor." He told us.

"Well, I guess that's my cue." Mrs. Ester said, and then

she back at me and smiled. "It was a real pleasure of finally putting a face with all the wonderful things my son said about you." She continued.

"Can I get another hug from you before you leave?" I asked her. Getting another hug from her wouldn't bring Sean back, but she's the next best thing to him.

"Absolutely," she said, and then she leaned and gave me another embrace. This time I held her tight because I knew that I'd probably never see her again. "Take care of yourself." She encouraged me.

"I will," I told her, and then we released each other. When she released her arms from her embrace, she reached into her purse, grabbed an ink pen and a piece of paper. Immediately thereafter, she leaned over my feeding table and scribbled a name and numbers down on it. I instantly assumed that it was her name and phone number. And when she stood back up and handed it to me, I realized that I was right. "Call me as soon as you have my grandchild, okay." She added.

On her way out of my room, she looked back at me once more and smiled. I smiled back and then she and Agent Saunders left.

Once my room door closed, I laid my head back on my pillow and started crying my eyes out. The fact of losing Sean to a gun battle and then to have his mother come to my room and show me so much love was overwhelming. Damn, I wished that I could see him again just one more time. I also hoped that I could get a do-over with Sean's sister Whitney. I can't figure out why she acted like she hated my guts. Okay, I can see why she's upset that she lose Sean because of a bullet that was meant for me. But like Mrs. Ester said, he died in the line of duty. Aside from that, I was lying in my bed, unconscious. I mean, come on, give me a break. I'm hurting too. I loved him just as much as she did. Maybe more. But I guess, loving him wasn't enough.

For the next hour or so, I just laid there, crying and thinking; thinking and crying. I was a mess. One of my nurses tried consoling me with inspirational quotes and bible verses, but it didn't work because as soon as she left out of the room, I broke down into tears again. I swear, I don't know how I'm going to get over Sean, especially now that I know I'm carrying his baby. I mean, who would've thought that I'd ever get pregnant? One part of me is happy to have a part of Sean growing inside of me. But the other part of me is sad because he won't be around to help me raise this child. I have no idea which way my life is heading from here, so all I can do now is pray that God watches over me and my little one inside me.

CHAPTER FOUR
Whitney Foster

Special Agent Saunders escorted my mother and me back to our car. Once we were safely back in the car and away from the FBI Agent, I opened up a dialogue with my mother about what had just transpired back in Lynise's hospital room. "Mommy, I don't know why you were so happy to meet that snitch back there," I commented. I was disgusted by the way my mother carried on in front of Lynise.

"Whitney, that's not nice. Don't call her that," my mother tried to chastise me. "And besides, she's carrying your brother's baby," she continued.

"You believe that, mommy? That could be the man's baby that kidnapped her." I chimed back in. "You should've told her that you knew all about it," I said sarcastically.

"I couldn't tell her that. She's been through enough."

"And why haven't?!"

"Whitney, I know you're hurt. But it's not her fault that Sean is dead, baby girl. So, you gotta' let it go."

"But I can't mommy! I love him so much!" I said as I began to sob.

My mother put her left hand on my right thigh and started rubbing it in a circular motion. "I know you do baby, I know you do….." she said and turned her attention towards the scenery outside the passenger side window. I knew that when she did this, it meant that she was talking to God in her mind. She's a very spiritual woman, so she talks to God in her mind all the time when she can't get any quiet time. When this happens, I make it my business to make her atmosphere as quiet as possible.

By the time we made it back to the hotel, she wanted to talk about Lynise being pregnant again. "I know you're having doubts about her having your brother's baby, but what if she really is carrying his baby? We can't turn our backs on her. Your brother would be heartbroken if that happens." She said as we walked onto the elevator of the hotel.

"Mommy, but what if she isn't?"

"I swear, you're just as stubborn as your father was," she commented, and she was right. My father was a very stubborn man, and when he believed something, no one could make him think differently.

"Don't forget that he was a wise man too."

"Only when it didn't concern you." She replied sarcastically as we walked off the elevator.

"Exactly," I replied as I followed her down the hallway

to our hotel room.

"I think you should give her a chance." My mother insisted.

"I don't like her. So, that's gonna be impossible."

"Just think about it."

Instead of giving my mother a response to her request, I let out a long sigh and rolled my eyes. She knows that when I do that, I'm totally against everything she's trying to drill in my head. I am 100% against anything that pertains to that chick Lynise. As far as I'm concerned, she could die, and I wouldn't blink an eye.

After we walked into our room, my mother took off her shoes and sat on the edge of the bed. I took off my shoes and climbed underneath my bedsheets. All I wanted to do at this moment was get a couple of hours of rest and get some food in my system after I get up. Anything outside of that wasn't a priority for me. Unfortunately for me, I couldn't say the same for my mother. She was on some other type of shit. She wants to save the world with Lynise in it. I see her wheels turning inside her head from the position I was laying in my bed. Lord knows what they could be. And in time, I'm sure they will be revealed.

CHAPTER FIVE

Lynise

When I woke up this morning, who would've thought that I was going to meet Agent Sean's mother. His sister too. But she doesn't count when it comes to pleasantries. His mother, however, made me feel like I was a part of the family. When she hugged me and told me that Sean called her and told her that I was his soulmate sent me over the moon. Her verbal gesture could not have come at a better time. Damn, that made me feel so good. Mrs. Foster was a nice lady and hopeful this won't be the last time I see her.

Now Agent Sean's sister is cut from a different cloth. She had it out for me the moment she saw my face. What had I done to her that made her treat me the way she did a few minutes ago? And to think that she blames me for Sean's death is heartbreaking. I hope and pray that she comes to her senses about this whole thing. Just like Agent Saunders said, "If he wouldn't have done it for me, then it would've been for someone else.

Several hours passed and, in that time, I was brought lunch since I missed breakfast and introduced to my new nurse named Jessica, who made her rounds a few times. Before the lunch tray was picked back up, I played around in the spaghetti and the fruit cup, but I managed to drink every ounce of the apple juice from the kid-sized circular container. I even had the new nurse to bring me two cups of crushed ice. I never knew this at first, but eating ice calms me. It gives me a sense of peace when I start feeling anxiety approaching. Why didn't I know this at first? This newfound remedy could've saved me from countless bouts of nervousness while trying to figure out the next step. Well, I guess now is better than never.

Devouring both cups of ice sent me to the bathroom three times, which of course was okay for me because I didn't mind getting out of bed. In fact, I wanted to get out of this fucking room. Looking at all four of these damn walls was annoying the crap out of me. And it felt like these walls were about to close in on me. I knew one thing, if I didn't get a chance to stretch my legs soon, I was going to go crazy. So, being the persuasive woman that I am, I figured that asking the agent outside my door couldn't cause any harm. I mean, what's the worst thing he could do? Tell me, no? So, in theory, I didn't have anything to lose. "Lynise, just do it!" I pushed myself, and then I walked over to the door. I grabbed onto the door handle and pulled it open. I wasn't surprised to see the agent in the hallway, but I was surprised to see that his back was facing me, and he was walking away from my door. I stood there and watched him as he walked towards the bathroom, which was four doors down from my room. At that very moment, I thought about racing towards the elevator and taking it down to the morgue where Sean's body was because I really needed to see him. It wasn't fair that everyone else got to see him but me. His mother made it clear that he loved me and that I was his soul mate. So, why not go and pay my last respects to him? They won't let me go to his funeral.

After mulling over how to handle this opportunity of a lifetime, I knew that if I was going to take the chance to see Sean, then I needed to do it now. Without wasting another second, I turned around and leaped into action. My heart began racing as I grabbed my clothes from a brown paper bag stored away in a closet next to my bed. In ten seconds or less, I managed to take off my hospital gown and slip on the same shirt, and a pair of shorts that I wore when I was brought to the belonged to that fucking serial killer. My shoes were also in that paper bag, so I slid those on my feet. "Come on, Lynise, you gotta go now," I urged myself because I knew my window of opportunity to get out of this room was closing at this very moment. So, knowing this, I darted over to the door, grabbed the doorknob and pulled it open slowly. Immediately after I opened the door, giving myself just the right amount of room to walk out, I was stopped in my tracks. "Going somewhere?" The nurse asked me.

"I was on my way to the nurse station to tell you that my toilet is backed up," I replied. I swear I don't know how I came up with that lie so damn fast. It just flowed freely from my mouth.

"Why didn't you use the call button? And why are you dressed?" She asked me as she walked by me to get into my room. Then watched her as she headed to the bathroom door.

"The call button wasn't working. And I peed in my hospital gown that's why I got on my clothes." I explained.

By this time, she was pulling the bathroom door open, so I followed her. I knew that as soon as she realized the toilet wasn't backed up, she was going to see that I was lying to her and she was going to throw a monkey wrench into my plans to get out of this room. I also knew that whatever I was going to do with her had to be done now before the agent comes back out of the bathroom.

"What are you talking about? This toilet isn't stopped up." She finally said after peering into the toilet from the entryway of the bathroom door. And when she took a step backward and turned around to look at me, I slammed a metal footstool into her face and knocked her down to the floor. Panic-stricken, I dropped the footstool onto the floor and grabbed the nurse by her arms and dragged her into the bathroom and closed the door shut.

"Please! Please! Please, don't let that agent be outside…" I whispered to myself as I hurried back to the door of my room. Luckily, when I peered into the hallway, there was no trace of him. There was no trace of anyone for that matter, so I took my chance and stepped out of my room, closed the door behind me and then I scurried down the hall. *Father God, please let me get off this floor before anyone catches me. All I want to do is see Agent Sean. That's it. And then I'll come back to my room without any resistance.* I prayed loud enough for only I could hear it.

After taking twenty-five to twenty-six steps, I managed to get to the elevator and get on it without anyone seeing me. I was a ball of nerves and the whole way down to the bottom floor of this hospital; all I could think about the nurse waking up and letting her colleagues and the agent know that I assaulted her. I hope she doesn't take charges out on me for hitting her. I mean, it's not like I did it purposely. All I wanted to do was leave my room for a few minutes so I could go and pay my last respects to Agent Sean, but then here she comes. What can I say, other than she was at the wrong place at the wrong time? I guess I will find out sooner than later.

When the elevator door chimed and opened, I took a deep breath, and then I let out a long sigh. "Come on; it's now or never." I encouraged myself, and then I stepped off the elevator. There was nowhere to go but left, so I started walking. I didn't have to walk far. There was only one door on this floor, so I tried to open it, but it was locked. That's when I realized that I had to press the button on the intercom pad located on the wall next to the door, so I pushed it. "What can I help you with?" I heard a man's voice say.

Scared shitless, I said, "I'm here to view the body of Agent Sean Foster."

"And you are?" He wanted to know.

"I'm a relative. I'm his sister…. Maggie Foster," I lied. I swear I don't know where that lie came from. I mean, it just came out of nowhere.

"His body has already been viewed by other relatives," He said coldly.

"I know my mother and sister have already been here. We drove in separate cars, so that's why they got here before I did." I said, hoping this excuse would get him to open the door.

"I'm sorry, but you're gonna have to wait to view his body after the Marshalls pick him up." He replied. And boy did this put a damper on my mood. I mean, I had just hit my nurse in the damn face with a footstool, dragged her into the bathroom and closed the door and snuck down here and this is the answer I get? No way. I've sacrificed too much up to this point to get rejected now.

"Sir, I beg you to let me see him. I drove all the way down here from Maryland in a separate car from my mother and sister because I don't get along with them. So, please let me see my brother for just a minute or two, and I will be out of our hair." I pressed him.

There was a long pause, and then he said, "Alright. But you've got two minutes max."

I almost jumped for joy after this man gave me the green light to see Sean. This was the best news ever. "Thank you so much!" I told him, and then he buzzed me to come in.

I entered a small room and found two chairs and a glass

41

window like you'd see in a check-cashing store, separating me from the room on the opposite side. After I stood there for a moment another a middle-aged, black guy dressed in a white coat appeared at the glass partition. "Show me your ID please." He instructed me.

Not prepared to do as he instructed, I stood there with a blank expression.

"I need to see your driver's license." He said.

"I'm sorry, but I left it back in my car." I lied once more.

"I can't let you in here without it." He replied.

"What is your name, sir?" I asked him in the gentlest way as possible. I was urging myself to come up with a good reason why I hadn't had my driver's license.

"It's Arnold."

"Arnold, please don't make me go back to my car. It's been a long drive, and I want to do is see my brother really quick. And then I'll be out of your way."

Arnold stood there quietly for a second. It was apparent that he was thinking about whether to let me in or not, so I applied just a little bit more pressure. "I'll be in and out," I assured him.

He turned and looked behind himself and then he looked back at me. "You have one minute." He finally said, and then he buzzed me in a second door near the glass partition.

I grabbed the door handle and pushed the door open. Arnold stood near the door and watched me as I greeted him. "Thank you so much!" I said after I came within arm's reach of him.

"Don't mention it." He replied, and then he watched me as I pushed the door close. "Make sure it's closed tightly." He instructed me.

After I shook the door handle to make sure the door was closed tightly, he told me to follow him. We walked a few steps and then off to the right was an entryway to a large room, and that's where I followed him. And what's so crazy is that as soon as I took the first step inside this room, I got an eerie feeling. It was a feeling you get when you see frogs dissected in glass jars on tables in your Science class. No wait, being in this room is far worse than seeing dead frogs in a glass jar.

"He's right over here." He said as he pointed to one of three bodies lying on a metal table in a black, zip-locked body bag.

Finally, being able to set my eyes on, Sean sent chills up my spine. I even got a sick feeling in my stomach. And then all kinds of thoughts started taking control of my mind as I followed Arnold towards Sean's body. Thoughts of him still being alive or my body lying in that black bag, instead of his. And then I started thinking about the possibility of our bodies lying down here together. Damn, I wished that I could turn back the hands of time. If I could, he would still be alive, and he and I would together at this very moment.

Immediately after Arnold and I stood next to the black body bag, he leaned over and unzipped it from top to bottom, and slowly, Sean's body was being revealed. I saw his face first. His eyes were closed, and he looked like he was fast asleep.

His chest was exposed next, and it was clear that he had been in surgery because there were gunshot wounds filled with blood all over that area. After surveying that area of his body, all different kinds of emotions flared up inside of me. "Those animals didn't have to shoot him these many of times," I commented as tears started falling from my eyes.

"I was told that he took every bullet that was meant for a young lady that he was protecting in one of the hospital rooms upstairs." Arnold started off saying, "He was one brave guy because I don't think that I would've been able to put my life on the line like that," he continued.

"That young lady he protected was me." I blurted out without even thinking twice about it.

Arnold's eyes grew in size. They were the size of fifty-cent coins. And as soon as he opened his mouth to say something, the buzzer button went off. I don't know how I did it, but I stopped sobbing at that very instance. It felt like my heart dropped into the pit of my stomach too. "That's probably for me." I managed to whisper as I grabbed onto his wrist.

"You gotta get out of here." He told me as he snatched his arm away from me. I could tell that he was severely irritated by me.

"Please don't let anyone know that I am here." I began to beg him.

"No, you lied to me." He protested as he started walking towards the front entryway of the room. I followed down behind him, and then he pulled onto his jacket so he couldn't leave the room.

"Please, Arnold, give me a chance to explain." I continued to beg him, trying to prevent him from leaving the room. And while I was trying to prevent him from blowing my cover, the buzzer kept going off.

"I've got to see who that is." He insisted while prying my hands from his white coat. And as soon as he removed my hands from one part of his jacket, I grabbed another part.

"If you don't release my coat I am going to scream." He threatened me.

I released his coat, but then I jumped in front of him and got down on my knees. "Please don't tell anyone that I am here. I beg you." I pleaded with him as I pressed my hands together like I was about to pray.

"Listen, lady, what you fell to realize is that you can't be in this room with me. I could lose my fucking job." He explained.

"I understand all of that, but some dangerous people are looking for me, and if they find out that I am in here with you, then you could be putting your life in danger," I explained to him.

"Exactly, and that's why I've gotta hurry up and get you out of here." He didn't mince words, and then he tried to walk around me.

I grabbed him by the hem of his coat and stopped him in his tracks. "The police are in on it too." I blurted out.

"What are you talking about?" He asked. He looked paralyzed for a moment as he searched my face for the answer to his question.

"The cops that were assigned to watch my room sold me out to the guys that were looking for me so they could kill me," I said, giving him only half-truths. I figured that I had to tell him something that would prevent him from selling me out. So, I only hoped that what I had just told him would decide against telling anyone that I was in this room with him.

He hesitated for a second, and then he said, "I knew I shouldn't have let you in here."

"I am so sorry." I apologized, all while still hearing the buzzer being constantly pushed.

"I know that I am gonna regret this but hide in that closet." He instructed me as he pointed to a closet door on the left side of the room. I jumped to my feet and made a dash for it.

As soon as I closed the door to the closet, I heard Arnold ask the person on the other side of the entrance to identify themselves. "I'm Special Agent Cross. I'm looking for a black woman. She's about 5'4, 130lbs., fair skin, with medium length hair. Have you seen her?" I heard the agent ask.

My heart was beating out of control while I waited to hear Arnold's response. "No, I haven't seen anyone of that description." He finally replied. And when I heard him say that, a heavyweight was lifted from my shoulders.

"Are you sure that you didn't see a woman of that description come down here? Because that same woman struck a nurse in the face with a heavy metal object and fled from her room. I was the agent assigned to safeguard her room when she escaped. She's a very dangerous woman, and she needs to be caught right now before she hurts someone else." The agent continued.

I swear, I wanted to come out of this closet and curse out that lying ass federal agent. Okay, I hit the nurse in the face, but I'm not dangerous. So, he needs to cut that bullshit out. Now I can only hope that Arnold doesn't fall into this agent's trap and keep his word to me.

"No sir, the last two people I checked in were the mother and sister of one of your own, Agent Foster. Aside from them, it's been pretty quiet." Arnold finally answered the agent.

"Well, if she comes down here, please call up to the 3rd-floor nurse's station."

"Will do," Arnold assured him. For the next 20 seconds, it went radio silent in this entire area. This only meant that Arnold got rid of the agent and was on his way back into the room where I was hiding.

I waited for him to come to the closet and tell me that it was okay for me to come out, but he didn't, so I opened the closet door and exited the closet on my own. As soon as I closed the door behind me, Arnold appeared. "I was wondering where you were," I whispered, making sure that no one could hear me outside of Arnold.

"Why didn't you tell me that you assaulted your nurse?"

"I didn't mean to do it. It was a mistake. She was trying to prevent me from leaving my room." I explained to him.

"Look, I don't want no problems, and I'm not trying to

lose my job so you might as well leave now before he comes back with more agents."

"Okay, I'm gonna leave, but can you do me one last favor?"

"What is it?"

"When you checked Agent Sean Foster's mother and sister in to see his body, where did their driver's license say where they were from?"

"I can't give you their information." He said without hesitation.

"Why not?"

"Because that's private information and it's against the hospital's policy."

"Please Arnold, all I wanna do is attend his funeral. That's it." I said, and then I pulled the paper out of my pocket containing Mrs. Ester's name and cell phone number on it. "Look, I already have her phone number. She just forgot to give me her address."

"Well, there you go. Call her and let her give it to you." He insisted.

"No, I can't. I want it to be a surprise." I pressed him. He could tell that I wasn't going to leave this morgue without getting her home address.

Arnold let out a long sigh, and then he said, "If you tell anyone about this, I will lose my job."

"I promise you that it won't happen. And when I leave here today, you won't ever hear from me again."

Instead of commenting, Arnold walked over to a desk that was only a few feet away from the closet that I hid in. I followed him. And as soon as he reached it, he leaned over, grabbed a sheet of sticky note paper and copied down the address he saw from the sign-in sheet on a clipboard sitting on his desk. After he copied the entire Maryland address, he stood up and handed me the notepaper and urged me to leave. "Now get out of here before someone catches you in here." He insisted.

I raced over to Sean's body, kissed him on the forehead, and then I scurried towards the door I initially came in.

"No.... you can't go out that way. Take the back door. It leads to the street." He instructed me.

"Thank you," I replied and made an exit from the back door that he escorted me to.

CHAPTER SIX

Whitney

I was sound asleep when my mother's cell phone started ringing. I watched her as she answered the call. "Hello," she said and then put the caller on speaker so I could hear who the caller was and the conversation.

"Mrs. Foster, this is Special Agent Saunders," The agent announced.

"How can I help you, Agent Saunders?" my mother asked him.

"I'm calling you because our witness Lynise Washington just fled from the hospital and my colleagues and I are curious to know if she mentioned anything to you about leaving or where she was going?" Special Agent Saunders wanted to know.

"Oh my, this is terrible news. But to answer your question, no, she didn't say anything to me about leaving that place. Are you sure no one kidnapped her again?" My mother inquired.

"Yes, we're sure that she wasn't kidnapped. Off the record, she assaulted her nurse before making a run for it."

"Oh no, is the nurse all right?" My mother wondered aloud.

"She only suffered a mild blow to the head. The doctor said she'd be fine."

"Have you guys looked at the surveillance cameras around the hospital." My mother asked.

"We're doing that as we speak." He replied.

"When did all this happen?" I interjected, not sure if the agent would hear me or not.

"This happened about thirty minutes or so ago." He answered me.

"Well, she can't be that far, especially if she's on foot." My mother chimed back in.

"She's from the area so we suspect that she may have had some help leaving that place," the agent explained. "But in any event, if she tries to contact you guys, please give me a call," he continued.

"Will do," my mother replied, and then they both disconnected the call.

My mother and I looked at one another in amazement. "Where do you think she went?" My mother asked me.

"Mommy, you know that I couldn't really care less," I replied sarcastically.

My mother sighed heavily. "I know you don't, but now

that I know she's carrying my grandchild, I'm concerned."

"Would you at least wait to see the baby before you start signing birth certificates?" I spat. My mother was really starting to irritate the hell out of me. I know it's just her and me so she would love to have a grandchild, but that bitch isn't the answer. I mean, come on, she was in witness protection. And according to my brother, she was snitching on some evil people. And those same people were the ones that took my brother's life. So, why should my mother even entertain that chick? She's bad news, and I knew that from the first time I laid eyes on her.

"Whitney, let's just give the young lady a chance." My mother said.

But I was 100% against it. "I'm not giving her anything. Wherever she is, that's where she needs to stay," I replied adamantly.

Instead of pounding the idea in my head that Lynise could be pregnant with her grandchild, my mother got up from the bed and went into the bathroom. Once again, I succeeded in getting her upset, but it wasn't my intentions. I just want her to open her eyes to what's really going on around her. That Lynise chick is no good, and I'm going to prove it to my mother. Now hopefully once that's done, she'd leave well enough alone.

While my mother was in the bathroom, my cell phone started ringing. When I took it off the night and looked at the caller ID, I realized that it was my boyfriend Jeff calling me, I answered it before the third ring. "Hi, baby," I said.

"What's up? Whatcha' doing?" He asked.

"Nothing really. My mom and I just got back to the hotel. I'm lying on the bed, and she's in the bathroom."

"Did you see your brother yet?"

"Yeah, we saw him. I cried a little bit as soon as I looked at him."

"How did your mama take it?"

"I'm surprised that she didn't cry at all. But I'm sure that as soon as she's alone, she's going to let it all out. That's what she did after my father died. But that's not it," I began to say.

"What...."

"You know the girl I told you that my brother was protecting when he got shot?"

"Yeah,"

"Well, me and mama met her. And while we were in her hospital room talking to her, the nurse comes in there and tells us that that ho was pregnant."

"No way!"

"Yes, way. And then on top of that, she had the nerve to tell my mother that she was carrying my brother's baby."

"Wait, didn't you tell me that she was a government witness?"

"Yes,"

"Then how could she be pregnant by your brother? Isn't that against the rules or something?"

"I said the same thing. Well, I actually said a lot of other stuff, but you get the picture."

"How many months is she?"

"I think she's like two months. But who's counting?!"

"You need to stop talking about that young lady like that. You know God don't like ugly!" My mother said after she walked out of the bathroom.

Jeff heard her voice in the background and said hello.

"Hello to you too," she replied. "Now, weren't you two just on the phone talking a couple of hours ago?" she continued.

"Yeah, but you know I've gotta keep tabs on her. I can't afford to let another man take her from me." He joked.

"Oh, stop it!" She chuckled.

"So, when are you coming back home?"

"We're heading out of here in the morning."

"Okay, so call me when you two get back on the road."

"I will," I assured him.

"Cool. I love you."

"Love you too."

CHAPTER SEVEN

Lynise

The moment I stepped out the back door of the county morgue, it felt like a burst of fresh air engulfed me. One part of me felt free, and then the other part of me felt like I was trapped. Trapped in a small cage-like a dog. I hated this feeling. I want to be free to roam around like no one is looking for me. I've been in some many near-death experiences that it weighs heavily on my mental state of mind. I do know that for me to move on with my life and not have to look over my shoulders, I'm gonna have to kill Bishop once and for all. Running from him starts today. And when it's all said and done, I will have either taken his life, or he will have to take mine.

The back door of the county morgue took me to a carport. It was apparent that bodies were dropped off and picked up at this location of the hospital. I knew that I had to get out of dodge before someone decides to pull up and see me leaving. I've risked a lot to get out of this hospital, so getting caught was not an option at this point.

From where I was standing, I could see that I was near the midtown tunnel off Brambleton Street in Norfolk. I knew that I couldn't walk through the tunnel, so I headed in the direction of Ghent which is an affluent area of Norfolk. I knew that the cops and the FEDS were looking for me to be in the area of the hospital, so I scrambled down Colley Avenue, making sure I stayed incognito. Walking in and out of a few restaurants on the strip helped me dodge all the cop cars I saw patrolling Colley Avenue. It seemed like every time I walked into a restaurant; a cop would drive by. My nerves were all out of whack. I didn't know if I was coming or going. While I was walking out of Starbucks, a young guy grabbed my attention by grabbing ahold of my arm. I immediately snatched it back from him. "What is wrong with you grabbing on me like that? I don't know you." I snarled at him after looking at him from head to toe.

He was a dark skin, medium built guy that was at least 5'11 in height. At first glance, he heavily resembled the rapper, Nas. Yes, he was that fine. But as soon as he opened his mouth, I knew that he was a man from the south. "I'm so sorry if I offended you." He apologized as his posture changed. He wanted me to know that he was genuinely sorry for grabbing my arm. "Please forgive me." He continued trying to defuse this situation.

"Yeah, a'ight! Just don't do it again." I warned him and then I turned around to leave.

"Can I buy you a cup of coffee?" I heard him say as I grabbed ahold of the door handle.

"No, thank you," I replied, and then I pushed the door open and walked out.

No soon as I released the door of Starbucks, I saw a cop car driving towards me. My heart collapsed into the pit of my belly, and without thinking twice, I quickly turned around and headed back into Starbucks. The guy was in line waiting his turn to place an order, so I walked towards him and stood in line behind him. I casually cleared my throat to get his attention. He looked back at me and smiled. "Had second thoughts?" He asked me.

"If that's what you wanna call it," I replied, giving him a half-smile, hoping that I could use him as a pawn if the cops happen to come in here looking for me.

"So, this means that you're gonna let me buy you coffee?" He wanted clarity.

"Yes, it does," I answered him, nervously looking over my shoulders every time I see movement through my peripheral vision.

He smiled, showing me his one-million-dollar smile. His teeth were something you'd see on a before and after the dental commercial. "Looking for someone?" His questions continued.

"No, but why did you ask?" I said nervously.

"Because you keep looking back."

"Oh, never mind that, I'm always looking over my shoulders. Been doing it for years."

"What's your name?"

"Ashley," I told him. I swear that name rolled off my tongue so fast, I didn't realize that I had said it until he repeated it.

He smiled once again. "Ashley, huh?"

"Whatcha' don't like my name?"

"I actually love it. It fits you."

"Well, what's your name?"

"Eric,"

"I guess, Eric fits you too."

"Live around here?" He wanted to know.

"Nope. My best friend does."

"Where are you from?" He pressed the issue. He was really trying to get to know me.

"I'm from Virginia Beach," I lied. I swear that was the first name I could come up with.

"So, where is your best friend?"

"She's still at work. I caught an Uber down here to hang out with her. But she had to work late today, so I decided to take a walk around her neighborhood and killed some time until she comes home." I replied, creating a real-life story. I noticed that lying as become so easy for me to do these last few months. Was it because I was living a lie?

"When you see your best friend, I want you to thank her for me."

"For what?"

"For allowing me to meet and spend this little time with

you."

"That's cute." I smiled and commented even though that pick-up line was whack ass hell. If only he knew that I was using his ass to get out of this jam I was in. I wouldn't be in his face otherwise. Okay, I will be honest and say that he was a very handsome guy. He resembled the young actor, Michael B. Jordan. He had the height, weight, facial features, facial hairs; you name it, this guy had it. He had the entire package, but the timing was off. If he would've caught up with me about a year and a half ago, I might've entertained him. Who knows?

Before he could comment, the Starbucks' employee welcomed us for stopping into the café, and then she asked us for our order. "I'll have the Salted Caramel Frappuccino, and she'll have....."

"I'll have the same thing." I chimed in.

He smiled at me. "Great minds think alike, huh?"

I smiled nervously and said, "I guess so."

The Starbucks clerk rung up our order and then Eric paid her. And while we were waiting for our beverages, we stepped to the side of the counter and started dialoguing. "So, Ashley, are you seeing anyone?" He started off.

I paused for second and thought about how I should answer this question. Technically I was single because the man I'm pregnant by just lost his life. But then again, I realized that my heart belonged to him, so where does that put me? Single? Or taken? "I'm between relationships." I finally answered.

"And what does that mean?" He probed.

"It means that I just got a relationship," I explained, but my heartfelt differently.

"How long ago was your breakup?"

"No disrespect, but can we talk about something else? Like where is your girlfriend? Or are you married?" I change the subject. He was making me feel really uncomfortable talking about Sean.

"Oh, I'm sorry," he apologized. "I will make sure that that never happens again."

"I appreciate it." I thanked him. "So, where is wifey?" I continued.

"I'm not married, nor do I have a girlfriend." He replied.

"You guys drinks are already," the Starbucks' counter clerk announced, and then she handed us our coffee. After we had our drinks in hand, we walked over to a nearby table and had a seat. Eric took a sip first. I followed a few seconds later.

"Now, where were we?" He asked.

"You were telling me that you were not married, nor did you have a girlfriend." I reminded him.

"Oh yeah you're right," he agreed and then he took another sip of his coffee. "So, have you ever been married?"

"I swallowed the mouthful of coffee, and then I said, "Unfortunately not."

"Kids?"

"Nope," I replied. "You," I continued.

"No,"

"Would you ever have kids?" I asked him, even though I could care less if you wanted kids or not. My main goal was to entertain this man as long as I could so I could hide out in the Starbucks café. I just hope that I can pull this off.

"Of course."

"Well, what's the problem? Why haven't you had any?"

"Because I haven't found the right woman to share that experience with."

"Have you been looking?"

"Not really,"

"Why not?"

"Because I'm gonna know her as soon as I see her,"

"So, what are you going to say when you see here?"

"I'm going to tell her that I've been waiting all my life to meet her."

"Oh, okay. I hear you loud and clear Mr. Casanova."
He chuckled. Trust me; I'm far from being Mr. Casanova."

"You could've fooled me," I commented, and then I laughed with them.

Eric and I talked for about 30 minutes. He told me that he'd been a personal trainer for five years to some very influential people in the Tidewater area. We even talked about his aspirations of moving out to LA so he could offer his services and build a celebrity clientele. And we talked about him possibly running for office in the political arena. I've got to admit that he is a well-driven man and he knows what he wants. Now when the tables turned, and I was at the end of answering the questions, I was more tight-lipped than he was, especially after he confessed to his interest in becoming a politician. I can't be socializing with a cat that wants to be a future mayor if his aspirations of wanting to be a celebrity fitness trainer don't work out. I wonder if he'd turned me in if he knew that I was on the run? I am seriously curious to know how he would play this whole thing out. Well, since I'm not a daredevil, I won't take the risk of telling him what I've got going on right now. My only hope now is to play it safe with him and be on my way as soon as that window of opportunity opens.

All in all, Eric knows that I am single, I don't have kids, and I lived in Virginia Beach. That was it. If I had said anything more, I'd risk the possibility of him finding out who I really am. I've got to protect myself against him. And I will do it at any cost.

Once we were done drinking our beverages, Eric stood up and deposed the empty cups in a nearby trash dispenser. "Whatcha' about to get into now?" He asked.

"I don't know. Why? You wanna hang out with me a little bit longer?" I boldly questioned him. I needed to engage him more so he could help me get out of this area before the FEDS spot me walking outside those doors. But at the same time, I didn't want to seem like I was sweating him either. I had to play it cool.

"I would love that." He replied, smiling from ear to ear.

"Well, let's go," I said and waited for him to lead the way.

Luckily for me, Eric's car was only 100 yards away from the front door of Starbucks. So from the moment, I stepped outside the Starbucks, I held my head down and allowed Eric to escort me to the passenger side of his black, Maserati Ghibli. I wanted to look over my shoulder to make sure that I hadn't been spotted, but I was too afraid to look up. After he opened the door, I slid in the car without hesitation. And when he closed the passenger side door, I looked over my shoulder and out the back window to see if my cover had been blown. The last thing I want is for the FEDS or US Marshals to snatch me up and take me back into custody. I was going to Sean's funeral with or without the FEDS permission and this guy Eric was going to be my ticket.

"Are you going to call your best friend and let her know that you're gonna hang out with me for a little while?" He asked me after he got in the car and started up the ignition.

"Where shall I tell her that I'm going?" I smiled at him.

"If you don't mind, we can hang out at my place." He suggested.

"And where is your place?" I wanted to know.

"About ten minutes from here."

"Well, I'll just tell her that when she calls me," I assured him, knowing damn well, I was lying my ass off once again. If only he knew that there was no best friend in my life. It's just me in these streets. "So, what are we going to do when we get to your place?" I wondered aloud. Because in my experience, when cats want to take you to their place, they only have one thing on their mind and that's sex. But in this case, that ain't jumping off. He's a nice-looking guy, and all, but my cookies belonged to

Sean. It doesn't matter that he's deceased. I'm pregnant with his child, so my body is off-limits. There's no if's, and's or but's about it.

"I thought we could talk more. Maybe watch a movie or something."

"Yeah, that sounds good. Let's do that." I agreed.

I watched the trees, the joggers and the people walking their dogs as Eric made his way down Colley Avenue. The day seemed so peaceful despite what happened earlier at the hospital. I can't say if it was because I was two steps closer to getting to Sean's funeral or was it because I was no longer under the strict supervision of the US Marshals. Whichever it was, I was fine and felt free. So that's all that mattered to me.

****

The drive to Eric's place took ten minutes like he had said. He lived in a new condominium complex called Westport Commons. After he parked his car in his assigned parking space in the large parking lot, he escorted me to the front door of his house. Immediately after he unlocked the door, he pushed it open. "After you," he said, and then he stood there and waited for me to cross over the entryway into his apartment. Now once I had done it, he came in behind me and then he closed the door and locked.

"Wow! This is nice." I complimented the living room area of his place. I was blown away after soaking up the interior design inside his apartment. From the custom sectional and the limestone fireplace in the sunken living room area to the colorful rugs and textiles, and artworks complemented one another. Even accented shelves accented brought life to the books and personal objects that adorned it. A meticulous layering of meaningful statues and framed pictures of his family brought in color and culture to the room. The whole room tied everything in perfectly.

"Tell me the truth," I started off saying, "you had someone help you decorate your place, right?" I continued.

He smiled bashfully. "Yeah, I did," he confessed.

"See, I knew it," I replied and then I took a seat on the sectional.

"Want something to drink? Bottle water? Sweet tea?" He offered.

"No, I'm good."

"A'ight, well I'm gonna run to the bathroom. If you need anything just holler."

"Will do," I told him and then I watched him walk away.

As soon as I heard the bathroom door close, I jumped to my feet and raced over to the fireplace mantel and took a look at everyone in the pictures he had posted up. First, I glanced at the older man and woman in the first with Eric in the middle. I knew instantly that they had to be his parents because he was the spitting image of them. The next photo I glanced at was of him and a couple of other guys. I could tell that they were at a bowling alley. There were more photos lined up on the mantel, but this last one caused me to look at it longer. It was a picture of Eric and a pretty white woman that seemed to be in her mid-twenties. She had long, blond, curly hair. She was a Britney Spears look-a-like. And the way he had his arm around her waist lead me to believe that she's either a good friend or an ex-girlfriend that he can't move on from. I mean, he did say that he was single, so who was this woman to him? Because this picture was telling me something totally different than what he told me earlier.

When I heard the bathroom door open, I knew Eric was on his way out of the bathroom, so I raced back to the sofa and sat down like I'd been there the entire time. "Wanna watch TV?" he asked me after he grabbed the remote from the coffee table and powered the television on.

"Yeah, sure," I replied.

"Anything, in particular, you wanna watch?" His questions continued as he sifted through the television channels.

"I'm cool with whatever," I said casually because I really didn't care. I was more focused on trying to figure out a way that I was going to get to Maryland so I can attend Sean's funeral. Anything outside of that was of no importance to me.

I sat there and watched Eric as he combed through over 50 channels until he finally stopped on the TV show Two and a Half Men with Charlie Sheen. He cracked a smile. "This is my favorite show right here." He said, and then he placed the remote control back down on the coffee table.

"I like it too," I admitted as I watched him take a seat on the sofa next to me. But in all honesty, I could care less. I was only talking because I needed to keep our dialogue going.

I noticed that while the show was running, we didn't talk much. But as soon as a commercial aired, he'd go straight into question mode. We spoke of him graduating from ODU, how he likes to cook, and we even talked about his favorite football team. The conversations were draining, but nevertheless, I kept a smile on my face. I knew my time was coming, but until then, I needed to be patient.

CHAPTER EIGHT
Whitney

An hour after I got off the phone with Jeff, my mother mentioned that she was hungry, so I offered to order Chinese food. She declined the offer and said that she'd rather get a Grill Shrimp Ceaser salad from the California Pizza restaurant across the street. "That sounds good. Let's go," I said. So, after we freshened up, we left the hotel and made our way across the street to the California Pizza restaurant.

Once we entered the restaurant, we were escorted to our seats. And after the hostess handed us menus, she took our drink orders and then she left the table. "Wherever Lynise is, I hope she remains safe." My mother mentioned.

"Mom, I'm really not in the mood to talk about her right now. Can we just have a nice lunch and talk about something else?" I begged her because I knew that I was going to say something she wasn't going to like, and from there it was going to turn into an argument. Right now, I just want things to be drama free, at least while we're eating.

"Okay, as you wish," she replied; and boy was I surprised. So, to keep things on a level playing ground, I sparked up a conversation about how we were going to organize Sean's repass. I knew it was only going to be close friends and what little bit of family we had on my dad side, but sorting out the details would still be a wise thing to do. Not only that, I figured that if I kept her mind occupied with matters concerning Sean the rest of our visit here in Virginia would be drama free. And that's what I did.

****

My mother and I hung out at the California Pizza restaurant for over an hour talking about things Sean and I did to get in trouble back when we were in grade school. We even talked about the time when my dad caught Sean kissing his first girlfriend in his bedroom when he was thirteen. Luckily for Sean, my dad found him in the act before my mother came home from work that day. My mother always said that if she had caught Sean kissing that girl, she would've embarrassed him and the whole school would've found out about it. I swear those were the times.

It took us less than five minutes to get back to our hotel room. We were in good spirits even though we have to bury Sean, but that all changed when we exited the elevator and noticed that two black men in suits were standing outside of our room. We got their attention once they saw us approaching them.

Both men smiled at us, and then they flashed their badges and told us that they were Federal Agents. "How can we help you?" My mother spoke immediately after they greeted us.

"Hi ma'am, my name is Agent Snow, and this is my partner Agent Cassidy, and we're here to assure your safety while you're in our jurisdiction." Agent Snow replied.

"So, you're saying that you're here at our hotel because you think that we're in danger?" My mother questioned him.

"Yes ma'am, that's exactly what I'm saying." He continued.

"Look, we don't need any protection from that girl. She's pregnant with my son's baby." She blurted out.

"How do you know that?" The same black Agent asked.

"When we visited her earlier, her nurse came into her room while we were there and told her the news." My mother explained.

I swear, if I had the courage to tell my mother to shut the fuck up I would've. I mean, why in the hell was she still so fixated that Lynise was pregnant by Sean? Why bring this is right now? But aside from that, I've already sized that ho up, and from what I saw lying in that hospital bed, she's no match for me. I would tear that bitch in half.

"And this happened today?" the same agent asked.

"Are you deaf? My mother just said it happened earlier." I interjected sarcastically. "And why don't you know this already? Agent Saunders was in the room too when the nurse announced it.

"My apologies but it sounds like that information was purposely redacted from our report, being that she was a government witness and he was the lead agent on that case." The other agent chimed in.

"Look, Agent, whatever your name is, my mother and I don't need bodyguards or protection from a pregnant woman. So, we would appreciate if you guys leave us alone. We have a long drive back to Maryland tomorrow morning, so all we want right now is some peace and quiet. Now can you accommodate that?" I added.

"Most certainly, but can we ask a small favor from you?" The agent said.

"That depends on what it is." I blurted out before my mother could answer.

He handed me a business card and said, "If by any chance Lynise contacts either of you, please give me a call at that number on the card."

"Yeah, okay," I said, and then I grabbed my mother by the arm and escorted her to the door of our room. I stuck the key card down in the electronic slot, and when the green light flashed, I pushed the door open, and then I escorted my mother into the room. Before I disappeared around the door, I looked back down the hallway and noticed that both agents hadn't gone anywhere. They were standing in the same spot my mother and I left them in after we ended our conversation. In one sense, it was creepy to see them still there, but then I figured that they probably wanted to make sure my mother and I made it into our hotel room before they left the floor. Whatever it was, I shook it off and closed the door.

Immediately after I closed the door, I slipped off my shoes and sat in the chair placed in front of the desk. "I cannot believe that they think she's dangerous and that she would harm us." My mother stated.

"No, what I cannot believe is that they think we need protection from her."

"Yeah, that's crazy. She's really a lonely soul looking for someone to love her."

"Mommy, I'm so sick of hearing you gloat about that woman. She's simply a reject that prayed on Sean's sympathy, and he paid for it with his death." I insisted. I needed my mother to see Lynise for who she really is and that's a low budget ho, in witness protection from people she did wrong. And because of her actions, my brother's life was taken. Never mind that he was doing his job. I know for a fact that if he weren't fucking her, then he would've made a better judgment call with his head and not his heart.

"Whitney don't talk like that. Your brother loved her. He told me himself."

"Believe me; it was lust, not love," I said adamantly.

Frustrated by my actions, my mother said, "There's no getting through that thick skull of yours,"

"Mommy, I'm just a realist."

"You need some compassion. That girl is pregnant, and she's roaming those streets alone. I only hope the agents find her before those bad people do."

"If I find out that the child, she's carrying is my brother's baby, then I'll be a little more compassionate towards her."

"I appreciate that," she replied and then she turned her attention towards the television.

For the next couple of hours, my mother played the silent game. It wasn't a shock to me because she always goes into silent mode when she feels like I'm being unreasonable. In my mind, I'm only trying to protect her. She is all I have left, and I will fight tooth and nail to keep it that way.

CHAPTER NINE

Lynise

It's been three hours since I've been at this guy's house. And it seems like the longer I am around him, the closer he tries to get. I mean, we started out with 30 to 40 inches between us. Now there's only 5 inches between us. And the weird questions he's asking me are becoming problematic. He's asked me if I like to kiss. Do I use my tongue when I kiss? And then he asked me what my favorite position was? I wanted so badly to say, dude, shut the fuck up! I'm not fucking you tonight or any other night. But then I realized that if I did scream on him, he'd put me out of his apartment at the drop of a hat. I also realized that if I didn't come up with a solid plan before the night's over, he's going to try to make his move on me and I can't let that happen.

"Hungry?" He wanted to know.

"Yes, I am. I was trying to wait on my bestie to call me and see if she wants to get something for the both of us before we met up, but she still hasn't reached out to me." I lied, adding another level to my fabricated story.

"Whatcha' got a taste for?" His questions continued.

"Pizza, maybe."

"From where? Papa John's? Pizza Hut? Dominos?"

"Let's call Papa John's," I suggested.

"Papa John's it is." He agreed and then he grabbed his cell phone from his pocket and dialed their number. "Whatcha' like on your pizza?" He asked me while the phone line rang.

"I'm just a plain cheese kind of girl. But you can add whatever you want to it." I insisted.

"I like plain cheese pizza too." He acknowledged, and then I heard a male's voice on the other end of his phone; that's how loud the volume on his cell phone was. "Thanks for calling Papa John's. Is this pickup or delivery?" He asked.

"It's delivery."

"Okay, go on with your order." The guy instructed Eric.

"Could I get a medium cheese pizza with a side of marinara sauce?"

"Would you like to add eight wings or a desert with that order?"

"No, thank you. The pizza is fine."

"Alright, a medium cheese pizza with a side of marinara sauce comes to $11.58. Will that be cash or charge?"

"Cash," Eric told him.

"Alright, your pizza should be delivered to you in the next 35 to 45 minutes." The Papa John's employee announced.

"Thank you."

"Thank you for calling Papa John's." the guy continued, and then they ended the call.

After Eric laid his cell phone down on the table, he stood up and told me that he had to go to the bathroom and that he'll be right back. I watched him leave the living room, and as soon as I heard the bathroom close for the second time, I grabbed his cell phone and started going through his text message. I need to know what kind of guy I was dealing with before I formulate a plan.

My heart rate picked up speed the second I had his cell phone in my hands. At first glance, I thought that he would have a password to unlock his phone, but he didn't. "Let's see what we have here?" I whispered to myself after I clicked on the link to open his text messages. The first name that popped up was Shelly, so I opened it. There was nothing significant about their text messages. And from what I can tell, she was a client of his just confirming their work out session that's happening the following day. The next text was from a guy he works out with named Quincy. Their dialogue was about getting together in a few days so he could show Eric a few new workout techniques. His mother texted him, saying that she loved him. And then I see a text from an attorney by the name of J.D. Thomas, Esq. saying that he's working on discrediting the woman accusing Eric of raping her. I swear, after reading this allegation, it made me sick to my stomach. I mean, what was the fucking world coming too? And why every time I turn around niggas are trying to force themselves on women? Was it hard for guys to get pussy nowadays? It can't be that bad where you gotta' sexually assault innocent women. I know one thing, if that bastard looks like he's going to try to rape me, I'm going to make him wish that he never met me and that this will be the last time he tries that sick shit with someone else.

When I heard the toilet flush and the door to the bathroom open, I backed out of his text messages and placed his cell phone in the exact place he left it before he left the room. I took a deep breath and exhaled so that I could collect my thoughts. I couldn't act like I'm mad when he entered back in the living room. He's going to know that something changed my mood and if he's smart enough, he may figure out that I went through his phone and read some of his text messages. I know from experience that niggas don't like when you go through their phones. I've seen a lot of chicks get their ass torn apart for going through their men's cellphones. And in this case, this guy isn't my man, so there's no telling what he may do if he found out that I was snooping through his text messages. "Act normal Lynise... you can do it. Don't let this nigga see you sweat." I said, my words were barely audible. I need this pep talk more than ever now because I was on foreign territory.

"I sho' can't wait for that pizza to get here." He commented as soon as our eyes locked on each other.

"I was about to say the same thing." I lied, forcing myself to put on a big smile.

"I'm getting myself a bottle of water.... want one?"

He asked me as he slightly turned his body and headed for the kitchen.

"Yeah, sure. Get me one." I replied because I was actually quite thirsty.

"One bottle of water coming up." He said cheerfully as he grabbed two bottles of water from his refrigerator. He returned to the living room less than a minute later. Immediately after he handed me a bottle of water, he sat down next to me. I opened my bottle of water while he was opening his book before he could consume a drop of it his cell phone started ringing. Without hesitation, he picked it up before it rang a second time. "Hello," he answered after he put the phone to his ear.

"Hi Chad, how are you?" I heard a woman's voice say.

"I'm sorry, but you have the wrong number." He quickly replied and disconnected the called.

"Are you okay?" I asked him after noticing his mood had changed.

"Oh yeah, I'm good." He replied and placed a cell phone back down on the coffee table.

"Are you sure? Because you look spooked." I pressed the issue, especially after hearing the caller asking for a guy named Chad. Was his name really Chad and not Eric?

"Yeah, I'm good." He insisted and then he grabbed the remote control and started sifting through channels again. This time he settled on watching a reality show called Shark Tank. He watched the entire episode in silent mode, and it was weird. I mean, we were just in conversations about every topic under the sun, but when he gets a phone call, and the caller asks to speak with a guy named Chad, he starts acting funny. So, why is that? Thankfully, the pizza delivery guy finally shows up at the front door with the pizza. Boy was I happy when he handed me a plate with two slices on it. "Enjoy," he said as he smiled.

It took he and I less than 10 minutes to eat both slices of our pizza. After he disposed of our paper plates, we continue to watch back to back episodes of the Shark Tank. On one of the episodes, a woman had an idea and prototype for a children's toy that she pitched to the sharks, and surprisingly she was offered one million dollars by two sharks. A single mother with two children and working at a dead-end job gets a chance to become a millionaire overnight. Now how often does that happen? In my world, probably never. So, to see this woman on national TV get this opportunity makes me realize that my life changed for the better. And all I have to do is make the first step. Get away from people that want to suck all the energy from my body. It was time for me to make a stand.

A couple more hours passed, and the night was winding down. And I was no closer to figuring out what I was going to do next until this fraud started making his moves on me. "I would sure like to get to know you better." He said while sitting next to me on the sofa. He was giving full eye contact. I was quickly becoming uncomfortable. But I knew that I had to stay calm and try to work this situation out as calmly as I could.

"I thought that was what you've been doing since we met at Starbucks," I mentioned while trying to remain calm. Didn't want to seem alarmed by his sudden aggression.

"I'm talking about getting to know you more."

"I chuckled nervously. "Trust me; there's not much more to know. I'm an open book." I assured him.

"I'm talking about getting to know the inner part of you. Hold you in my arms to get a sense of how soft you are, and then I wanna kiss you on the lips to feel how soft that are." He said boldly as he leaned in towards me.

I started leaning back slowly to prevent him from trying to kiss me. "Hold up, wait a minute, you're moving just a little too fast for me," I told him, at the same time using my arms to block him for getting any closer to me. Unfortunately for me, that didn't work. He leaned in further towards me until my back was firmly planted against the leather cushion of the sofa.

"Eric, I think you're moving too fast for me. Can we talk just a little more? You know, go on a date first because I'm not the type of girl who gives up the panties only after spending a few hours with a guy I just met." I explained.

"Let me just get a kiss." He pressed forward while trying to move the arms away from my face.

"No, I am not. So, please stop." I told him while trying to push him off of me.

"Okay, I'll stop if you give me one kiss." He tried to compromise with me.

"No, I am not kissing you. So, please stop." I spat. My blood pumping through my veins started boiling now.

"And whatcha' gon do if I don't?" He snapped. I swear,

this negro switched from Dr. Jekyll to Mr. Hyde in a millisecond. His face was horrifying. His eye grew five inches in size while the veins in his forehead protruded. They looked like they were about to burst.

"Look, Eric, please don't do this. You seem like a nice guy. And……"

"And what?" He interjected.

"Could you please just let me up."

"I'll let you up if you give me a kiss." He insisted. He was making it clear that he wasn't going to let me up until I kissed him. I had no other options.

"Look, Eric, I am not giving you a fucking kiss! Now get the fuck off me!" I roared as I began to push him away from me because I had had enough of trying to be nice to him.

"Shut the fuck up! You fucking tease!" He growled. His face was menacing. But the strength behind his arms and hands proved to be more fierce. And before I knew it, he covered my nose and mouth with both of his hands and began to smother me, trying to cut off all of my oxygen. "Now look at what you made me do! All you had to do was give me a fucking kiss. But no, you planned to come back to my place and tease me like a little whore." He snapped, adding more pressure to my face.

"N…..n…..n….no….n…." I tried to say, but he muffled my words every time I spoke. I was also losing consciousness and my will to fight this guy. But then I realized that this wasn't just about me. There was a little pint size fetus inside of me — Sean's baby, which was more than enough reason to fight for he or she too. Now, I had to figure out how to outsmart this maniac before he fucked around and snatched my life from me. *Stop fighting him back. Act like you're giving up. Just fall limp.* I thought to myself. And what do you know, fifteen to twenty seconds after sub coming to his demands, he released some of the pressure he had penetrating my nose and mouth. Breathing the air around me was becoming better by the second. I coughed a few times between every inhale and exhale.

"Are you done with being a tough girl?" He asked me. He was laying on the tough-guy image really thick.

"Yes… yes, I am." I replied, I needed to convince that I wasn't going to give him any more problems, even though I had other plans for him.

"Well then, be a good little girl and give me a kiss." He demanded. I swear, on a stack of Bibles I was not trying to kiss this rapist-killer. He was disgusting.

"I'll tell you what, if you let me get up and freshen up a little bit, I promise to give you more than that kiss you're asking for." I got up the gumption to say, perking my lips the whole time.

"If I let you up, you aren't gonna do anything stupid are you?" He questioned me. There was no question that he was somewhat suspicious of me.

"I promise that I won't do anything other than freshen myself up and then we can go to your bedroom and do whatever you want." I tried to assure him. I mean, I gave him the most sincere expression that I could muster up. I needed this guy to believe me because otherwise, I probably wouldn't make it out of here.

He stared at me for a moment, like he could read my mind. I honestly didn't know if he was going to start choking me and smothering my face again or let me get up from this sofa. My heartrate quadrupled while I waited for Eric to make his decision. I was literary at his mercy.

"Now, I'm gonna let you get up and go to the bathroom. But when you come out, I want you naked. You understand me?" He said wickedly.

"Yes, I understand," I told him.

Eric slowly crawled off me but gave just enough room for me to get up from the sofa. Once I was standing up on both feet, I thought to make a run for the front door, but then I remembered, that I was already on the run so where could I go? And that's when it hit me. I figured that if I could convince him to go to his room, get naked and wait for me in his bed while I was freshened up, and when I return, we could partake in a little bit of role-playing. I tie him up, put a gag in his mouth. We'll do all the shit sex slaves do when they engage in sexual bondage. But I've got to make it crystal clear that I must tie him up first. And when I'm done with him, I will allow him to turn the tables on me. Now, I can only help that he takes the bait.

"Let's do something fun." I started off saying…

"What's on your mind?" He replied after he stood up from the sofa. We were standing face to face.

"I thought that it would be fun if we dabbled in a little bit of sexual bondage. You know, you tie me up and pour hot candle wax on my back. Then I tie you up, and you watch me while I bite you the tip of your chest nipples and suck on your dick." I continued.

He instantly became giddy. "Now, you're speaking my kind of language." He commented.

"Well, let's get down to it," I instructed him seductively.

"I'm ready," he announced as he rubbed his hands together in a circular motion.

"Let's go," I insisted and grabbed him by the hand, but he led the way to his bedroom. As soon as we crossed the threshold into his room, I started taking off my clothes. I wanted to show him that I was getting ready to show him the best time of his life.

"I love your enthusiasm." He stated as he stood there and watched me disrobe.

"Well, if you love it so much, why don't you take off your clothes too," I told him and then I bit down on my bottom lip softly.

"Roger that!" He commented and started taking off his clothes.

"Take off your boxer shorts too so I can see what I'm working with." I insisted.

Within a flash, he slipped off his underwear and revealed a six-inch penis that had the width of a Sharpe magic marker. His dick was insanely small; which is probably why he can't get a chick to have sex with him. I was turned off, but somehow I managed to keep an enthusiastic smile on my face.

After taking off all my clothes except for my bra and panties, I stood there with my hands on my hips and asked him if he had a couple of sets of handcuffs? I thought he would become suspicious about why I wanted them, but to my surprise, he didn't mention it. In fact, he the extra mile by grabbing four sets of metal handcuffs from a shoebox that was stored away in his closet. "Here you go." He said and handed all the handcuffs to me.

"Do you have any wax candles?" I asked him while I grabbed the handcuffs from his hands.

"Yep, got a couple of them in the bathroom."

"Would you get them for me?" I asked him.

Like a kid in the candy store, this overgrown as man skipped his dumb ass to the bathroom and came back with two candles. "Got 'em." He stated, his mood became more jovial than it was when I first suggested to partake in a bondage sexual encounter.

I placed them all on the edge of the bed and instructed Eric to lie back and spread his arms and legs. Like a dummy, he did just that, and I had his wrists and ankles handcuffed to the head and footboard of the bed. "Wait a minute; I'm missing something," I mentioned while looking at Eric lying there handcuffed.

"What's wrong? What are you missing?" He wanted to know.

"I need a blinder for your eyes and gag for your mouth."

"I don't have either of those."

"This is not going to work then," I told him in a disappointed manner.

"Why don't you use one of my handkerchiefs. I have over a dozen of them in the top left drawer." He suggested.

Suddenly in better spirits, I said, "That'd be perfect."

When I looked in his dresser drawer, I noticed that there were a ton of handkerchiefs in all different colors. But I wasn't interested in the number of colors he had; I was more concerned about how big they were. And after realizing that they weren't big enough, I grabbed two of them and immediately tied them together. "Ready to have some fun?" I asked him, knowing that I was about to make him wish that he never met me.

"You damn right I'm ready." He replied.

"Alright, well let's get this gag on you so the party can begin," I said with excitement but trying my best not to vomit in my mouth. I mean, this sicko really believed that I was about to play sexual games with him. Was he really off his rocker?

****

With him bound and gagged, I definitely had the upper hand over him. "Before things begin, let me say a few things." I started off while picking his pants up from the floor. I grabbed his wallet from his back pants pocket and started going through it. He only had eighty bucks in it, but I took it anyway and waved it in the air. "Just so you know, I am going to take this little bit as money, and I might take your credit cards too," I said and pulled an American Express gold card from the credit card from the cardholder compartment of his wallet. But when I looked at the name, and it read Chad Miller, I was literally taken aback. "Wait, what the fuck……" I said in almost a whisper like way as my heart beats began to pick up speed. I pulled his driver's license from his wallet next. And what do you know, the name Chad Miller was printed on that as well.

Searching further through all the compartments in his wallet, I pulled out a small clipped newspaper article. After unfolding it, and getting a clear view of it, the title of it read: Chad Miller, CEO of a Plumbing Company, is accused of raping a woman during a follow-up visit to her home was arraigned today and entered a not guilty plea. The trial has been scheduled for Dec. 2, 2019. Sick to my stomach, I stormed back into his bedroom with the newspaper article in my hands. His nearly popped out of his eye sockets when I flashed the black and white paper article before him. "So, your name is real is Chad Miller, huh?" I roared. My volume escalated quickly. And since he couldn't answer because of the gag in his mouth, I spoke for him. "You fucking liar! 'Round here acting like your name is Eric. I knew something was wrong when that person on the phone asked to speak to Chad, but then you lie and tell the person that they had the wrong number." I spat. My adrenaline was pumping rapidly. And without thinking twice about it, I reached down and smacked the shit out him. His skin color instantly turned red.

"I swear, I wanna kill you right now you fucking coward! What gives you the right to rape women?" I screamed at him. "Now I know why you told me your name was Eric. You're a fucking disgrace to your mother. Fucking asshole!" I continued, and then I punched him in his face. He flinched as soon as my fist connected with his face.

"Guess what I am going to do?" I started off, like I was asking him another question, "I'm taking your car since I've got somewhere to go. And I'm taking this little bit as money you got in your wallet too. I mean, it's not like you're going to need it. Because you're going to be lying here until someone becomes worried and starts to look for you, but if they don't, then you're going to be fucked! I hope you don't have to use the bathroom, you fucking scum of the earth." I said, and then I spit a massive glob of my spit in his face. I wanted to let this psycho know that he fucked with the wrong chick.

"You know what dummy? My real name is Lynise, and I'm a bitch from the hood! As a matter of fact, the FEDS are looking for me. See you thought that you were going to bring me to your house and do whatever you want to me like you did to this poor lady in this article. But I played your stupid ass. And don't try to deny it. I saw the text message that your lawyer sent you. And while I think about it, he ain't worth shit either. Talking about, he's going to find ways to discredit that woman. Men like y'all need to be shipped to an island by yourselves so that you can rape one another. See how you like it then." I said, gritting my teeth at him.

While I was screaming on this imbecile, I had become more irritated by the sight of him. I started thinking about when he someone finally rescues him; he's going to regroup and start prowling the streets for his next victim. That thought gave me a sick feeling, and this influenced me to do something harmful to him. I wanted to inflict pain on him like he's done to other women. I also wanted to leave a mark on his psychotic ass too. But what, though? What could I do to him? And that's when it hit me to burn a layer of skin in his crotch area. Burn the pubic hairs around the groin area too. I'm going to make sure he'll never try to rape another woman.

I left the bedroom and headed into the kitchen. I was specifically looking for a fluid or cigarette lighter and found one as soon as I opened one of the utility drawers next to the drawer where he kept his silverware. Without delay, I raced back in the bedroom. When Chad saw me carrying a yellow, ten-inch, plastic handle, multi-purpose lighter he started fidgeting in the bed. Moving his arms and legs, hoping to break away from the cuffs. He looked very alarmed.

"Don't get scared now, nigga! I'm about to teach you a valuable lesson." I warned him as I approached him. I walked around to the right side of the bed, leaned over towards his groan area, flicked the lighter, and then I held it underneath his scrotum. The hair and flesh from his skin started frying, and Chad was going mad. He was turning into a beast as he rocked the bed back and forth. At one point, I thought he was going to break out of the handcuffs. That's how intense he was acting. "Ugggg….ugggg….ugggggg," was all he could utter from the mouth gag. His eyes were bloodshot red, and they were watery too. I knew that if he could get out of those cuffs, he would kill me without hesitation.

"This doesn't feel too good, huh?" I asked him while turning my nose up to him. The sight of him sickens me. "I'm gonna make sure you don't use your dick to rape anyone else," I vowed all while I was still burning parts of his groan area. But once I burned all of his pubic hairs and fried the first layer of his skin, I threw the lighter on his bed and said, "I hope you never get laid again, you fucking piece of shit!"

All I heard back was this moron were sounds of grunting, agony, and pain. He was also crying like a baby. "Bye, you fucking coward!" I said, and then I left him wallowing in his own misery. And now that my job was done, it was time for me to get the hell out of dodge before someone comes here looking for Chad, being that Eric wasn't really his name.

Thankfully it was nighttime when I walked out of Chad's place. From what I could see, there was no one standing outside nor looking out of their windows when I got into Chad's car and drove away.

While on the road, it quickly dawned on me that I couldn't drive his car all the way to Maryland. I'd probably get pulled over before I could cross stateliness. So, I needed to find another vehicle and do it fast. And that's when I decided to take this car over to the chop shop Feather-in-Fins' fast food restaurant off Princess Anne Road. I knew a guy that ran it by the name of Mitch, and he could take this car off my hands with the quickness.

It took me less than fifteen minutes to get there. And

immediately after I pulled up in the industrial parking lot, I saw the warehouse and the junk cars that surrounded the establishment. But there was a problem., there was a 12-foot gate with bob wires that protected the salvage yard, and the gate was locked. "Fucked!" I hissed looking at my dilemma from the driver seat of the car. "What am I going to do now?" I said out loud while trying to figure out what I was going to do. I knew that I couldn't ride around in this car for fear of being stopped by the cops. And I've got to keep in mind that anyone could rescue Chad at any given time. I mean, he could have a housekeeper, or he could have a mother that has a key to his apartment that routinely shows up every day at the same time. Whichever the case, he could be set free, and the hunt for me would ensue.

"I guess it's gonna be a long night," I uttered quietly, and then I turned off the ignition and laid my head back against the headrest.

****

The night seemed long while trying to endure the rainstorm that never seemed to want to go away. I found myself turning the ignition on and off to soak up some of the air condition, being that the constant rain caused a tremendous amount of humidity and heat to circulate the inside of the car. And every time I looked at the time on the dashboard of the car, it seemed like it never moved. I was miserable as hell.

Now I can't tell you how I finally shut my eyes, but when I heard a knocking sound, it scared me awake and for the first time I felt a sense of relief. Hunched over and looking into the driver side of the window was a very familiar face, so I rolled down the window that instant. But he beat me to the point and started talking first. "Why are you parked outside this gate? You know this is private property?" He made me aware, and he didn't seem to happy about it either. Mitch was a fine ass nigga. He was a cloned version of the actor Morris Chestnut, but a little shorter in height. Everybody in the Tidewater area knows that Morris is the man to go to when you want to make some extra money selling hot cars. You can also go through him to get things off the black market too. Besides selling and buying goods from him, he's also a lady's man. So far, no woman can seem to lock him down and make him a married man. Plus, I heard he's got over a dozen kids; most of them by different women. In addition to the harem of woman he's got on speed dial, he's got some real estate property; a couple of four-unit apartment buildings and two-unit duplexes in the sections of Norfolk. Word around town is, that's where his children live with their mamas. Talk about having *in-house pussy*!

"Mitch, it's me Lynise. Remember you used to come to the strip club where I bartended at?" I replied, trying to job his memory.

He leaned in further towards me to get a better look and then he stood straight up. "Oh yeah, you're involved with that FED shit. And you have a lot of people up in arms about it too. I hope you know the Carter brothers put out a heavy bounty on your head." He warned me.

"Yeah, they tried to off me at the hospital a couple of

days ago."

"I know. I saw that shit on TV. But the news people didn't mention that you were the target. They said that a federal agent got killed."

I let out a long sigh. "Yeah, they got that part right."

"Well, you better be careful because if I was a grimey ass nigga, I could easily make a call and collect on that bounty."

"That's why I'm here because I know you ain't a grimey nigga." I started off, and then I said, "Check this Maserati out. It's nice, huh?"

He took a couple of steps backward and gave it a 10-second look. "It's a'ight," He finally said nonchalantly. I knew what game he was trying to play. He didn't want to seem eager to take the car off my hands. This way would allow him to low ball me just in case I was trying to sell it.

"Look, I just took this car off this nigga that took me back to his house and tried to rape me. Now, I'm trying to leave town, but I can't get on the highway with this car, so I was wondering if you could give me a couple of grand for it and a car that would take me 500 miles without breaking down." I explained.

"You didn't kill that nigga, did you?" He asked me, giving me a skeptical look.

"No, but I fucked him up pretty bad," I assured him.

"Hey....yo'.... I don't want no details. Just drive the car in the warehouse after I unlock the gate." He instructed me, and then he walked away from the vehicle.

I drove the Maserati inside the gate and then inside the

warehouse. After I parked the car and turned off the ignition, I was amazed at all the cars I saw parked inside this place. There were at least thirty cars in here and out of that thirty, twenty of them were foreign cars, and those foreign cars were on car lifts. The inside of this warehouse looked like something you'd see in a movie. It was that insane.

"Come into my office." I heard Mitch yell from the 200-feet away.

I saw him disappear behind a door, so headed into that direction. The entrance to the office was open, so I walked in. Mitch was sitting behind his desk, counting money that I assumed came from an opened metal, petty cash box that was sitting on his desk. "Have a seat." He insisted.

"No disrespect but I ain't trying to get comfortable. My goal is to get in and out of this place and be on my way." I said respectfully.

"A'ight, well where are the keys to the car?" He asked me while still counting the money in his hands.

I placed the Maserati keys on the desk.

"Here's two grand." He said and plopped down a stack of one-hundred-dollar bills down on the desk in front of me.

I grabbed the money from the desk. "Whatcha' giving me to drive?" I wondered aloud while stuffing the dough down into my pants pocket.

Mitch went into a drawer behind his desk and pulled out a set of keys. He held them out for me to grab from his hand. "These keys go to a 2002 Honda Accord. There are over

200,000 miles on it, but it still runs good, and it's gonna take you a long way."

"Come on now, Mitch, a 2002 with over 200,000 miles...." I whined with disappointment.

"Don't worry; it won't break down on you." He tried assuring me.

I hesitated for a moment, and then I reluctantly said, "Alright. Show me where it is."

"Let's go." He replied and led me out of his office and out of the warehouse. The 2002 Honda Accord he was giving me was parked a few yards outside the side door of the warehouse. At first glance, the exterior looked okay. I just hoped that it worked.

"The tank is full, so you won't have to stop and get gas." He stated as he walked with me towards the car.

"I appreciate that..." I said as I opened the driver side door.

"What do you think?" He wondered aloud.

"It's clean," I said while looking around the interior. On some real shit, the interior was to be expected for a 2002 vehicle. All he did was vacuum the floor, cleaned the windows, and wiped down the upholstery; nothing more.

After I started up the ignition. Mitch leaned into the driver side window and said, "Be careful out there. We're living in a cold, cold world. So, wherever you're going when you leave

here, make sure you stay there because those niggas that want you dead ain't gonna stop looking
 for you until it's done."

"I know."

"Well, get out of here and don't look back."

"Thanks for helping me. I really appreciate it."

"Don't mention it. Now get out of here." He said, and then he watched me as I drove away.

CHAPTER TEN

Whitney

My mother and I took a shower, got dressed, grabbed our things and then we checked out of the hotel. While we were putting our stuff in the car, my mother noticed that we were being watched by two men in a black GMC SUV parked across the street from the hotel. We couldn't see their faces after she pointed them out because the tint of the truck was really dark. But the silhouette of their bodies was definitely visible. "So, they found a way to watch spy on us after all." My mother commented after she crawled in the passenger side seat of the car.

"Better out here than inside the hotel with us," I commented after I got in the driver seat and closed the door behind me. I purposely drove by the SUV and looked directly at the driver through the tinted window, so he'd know that I knew he was watching me. After I rolled my eyes at him, I sped off and headed towards Highway I-64. I figured the sooner I get out of Virginia, the less I would have to worry about the fucking FEDS watching me and my mother like a hawk.

"When I get back home, I'm gonna call your Aunt Beverly and your Uncle Glenn and let them know that we're back. I know Beverly will want to come over as soon as we cross stateliness. So, I may wait a couple of hours to call her."

"Did you get the chance to call the funeral arrangement coordinator yet?"

"Not yet. I planned to call him as soon as we get back to Maryland."

"I wonder how long it's gonna take them to bring Sean's body back home," I wondered aloud.

"Remember we asked Agent Saunders yesterday and he couldn't give us an answer," My mother pointed out.

"I remember. It irritated me too. Did you notice that every time we asked one of those agents' a question, they either said that they didn't know, or no one told them?" I commented. I was referring to the fact that only a few agents knew that Lynise and Sean were having an affair and on top of that, no one bothered to tell the agents we saw yesterday that she couldn't be a threat to us because she's now pregnant. There's a weak link somewhere, and it needs to be eliminated. And I mean, A.S.A.P.

****

One hour into my drive I saw the same black SUV following me. This alarmed me at first minute, but then it made me angry.

I started not to say anything to my mother about it, but then I decided against it because I was feeling enraged now. "Mommy, those agents are literally following us."

"What are you talking about? Who's following us?" She asked me and then she looked over her left shoulder. She couldn't see out of the back window because she couldn't quite see over the back seats.

"The agents. The ones that were sitting in the tinted SUV when we were leaving the hotel," I explained.

"You said they're following us?" She wanted clarity.

"Yes….. they are four cars behind us. You know what? I'm gonna get off this next exit and make them follow me to a gas station and curse their asses out." I spat.

"Whitney, watch your mouth around me." My mother chastised me.

"Mommy, I'm sorry. I'm just tired of these cops crowding my space even after we told them that we don't need them."

"Just keep driving. I'm sure they'll back out of us as soon as we hit the Maryland state line." My mother reasoned.

I let out a heavy sigh, and then I press down on the accelerator harder after realizing that my mother could be right. Maybe they are trailing us because they want to make sure we got out of Virginia safely. In my opinion, I didn't think that we were in danger, but if they're going to waste taxpayer's money on gas, then so be it. I know one thing though, if I see them parked outside my mother's house after we get in the house, then there's going to be problems between them and me. And I won't back down this time.

Three hours into the drive back to Maryland, I noticed that that black SUV that the feds were driving had stopped falling us. I can't say when they stopped following us, but I can tell you that it was a huge weight lifted from my shoulders. I hate when I don't have control over situation concerning me. It sends me into a tail spend, and it gives me anxiety, which are two things that I don't like dealing with. All and all, I'm just glad that those assholes found something better to do besides follow my mother and me back to Maryland.

I was happy when I pulled up to the house and seen my boyfriend Jeff's Acura RLX parked in the driveway. I needed so badly to see him after everything I've been through while my mother and I were taking care of my brother's business back in Virginia. I had a ton of stories to tell him and just hope that he's up for it. "I am so glad to be home." My mother stated after I parked my car in the driveway next to Jeff's car.

"So am I." I agreed with her after I shut off the engine.

"Glad you ladies are home," Jeff said after he walked out onto the front porch to greet us. My heart fluttered instantly.

"Not more than I am." I insisted as I grabbed me and my mother's overnight bag from the back seat of the car. My mother walked ahead of me. After I closed the back door of the car, I followed suit.

My mother had already gone into the house by the time I reached the porch, so there was plenty of space for him to embrace me. The warmth of his body made me realized that there was nothing better than being in the arms of a man that loves you. His touch made me feel protected, and it gave me the sense that family was everything. "How was the drive?" He wanted to know after he released me from his arms and took the overnight bags from my hands.

"It was alright until I noticed that my brother's agent buddies were following me home. But when I crossed the Virginia and Maryland stateliness, they turned around."

"You're acting like that was a bad thing." He said and led me into the house.

"Well, you just had to be there to witness their incompetence behavior. And to add insult to injury, they didn't know how to back off when I told them that me and my mother didn't need them to babysit us." I explained after I entered the house.

Jeff sat our bags down on the living room floor and joined my mother in the kitchen. I realized that she was boiling a pot of water for a cup of tea when I entered the kitchen behind Jeff. "Don't believe anything she's telling you. Those agents were nice and accommodating."

"She's only saying that because they let her meet Sean's alleged baby mama," I interjected sarcastically and sat down on the barstool next to the kitchen island. Jeff sat down next to me after he grabbed a coffee mug from the kitchen cabinet and placed it down on the counter next to my mother's coffee mug.

"How is her personality?" Jeff wanted to know.

"She's really nice, especially under the circumstances." My mother spoke up first while standing by the stove.

"I believe she was putting on an act in front of mama."

"No, she wasn't. Jedd, you know I'm a good judge of character, and all I saw was a woman who's misunderstood and looking for someone to love her. And I believe that Sean provided that for her." My mother reasoned as she looked at Jeff the entire time.

"Is she coming to the funeral?" Jeff asked, looking at us both.

"She wants to, but Sean's colleagues said that it's against their policy being that she was in witness protection." My mother replied.

"And thank God for that." I blurted out sarcastically.

"Come on, baby, be nice." Jeff eased in the conversation. He knows that I don't play and will put him in the doghouse if you go against anything I say. But when it comes to my mother, he always finds a way to fall in the gray area.

"I've been telling her that for the past couple of days." My mother interjected as she took the pot of water off the stove and started pouring it into her and Jeff's mugs.

"Have they figured out when the funeral was going to be?" Jeff changed the topic.

"They haven't given us a date yet," I replied.

"One of the agents said we'd get a call about the date anywhere between today and tomorrow." My mother added as she dropped a tea bag in her and Jeff's coffee cups. Seconds later she handed Jeff his mug. He thanked her and turned his attention back towards me.

"Are they going to bury him in one of those government ran cemeteries?"

"Yes, that's what we were told," I told him.

"I wished they would bury him where dad is," I mentioned.

"Yeah, I wanted that too." My mother agreed, and then she took a sip of tea from her coffee mug.

"Man, I swear I can't believe that Sean is gone," Jeff stated and then let out a long sigh. "I'm gonna miss spanking him on the basketball court." He continued.

I chuckled. "He said that the only reasons you beat him was because you always cheated." I blurted out.

"What about the shouting matches you two used to have during the super bowl? You two used to be in each other's faces during the whole game, but as soon as it ended, you two would be best friends again." My mother interjected.

Jeff chimed in and reminisced about other things he and my brother Sean did, and it was refreshing to hear about the love Jeff had for Sean. I sure wished that I could turn back the hands of time. But since that won't happen, my brother will surely be missed.

CHAPTER ELEVEN

Lynise

With the $2,000 in cash and a 2002 Honda Accord to take me from plan A to plan B, I was in a better position than I was 12 hours ago. Now all I can think about is getting to Maryland so I can attend Sean's funeral. I know that I can't stand out in the opening because if I'm caught, they'll take me back into their custody. And I'm over the witness protection program. It's been a disaster since I first agreed to help them bring Bishop down less than six months ago. Not only do I have to watch my back from the niggas the Carter brothers commissioned to kill me, but I've also got to watch my back from Bishop and the niggas he's ordered to kill me. When it's all said and done, I want to be able to go somewhere far away and live my life on my terms and never look back at this God-forsaken place. But first, I must close this last chapter of my book.

As soon as I jumped on the Highway I-64 West, it felt like a weight was lifted from my shoulders. I knew that I wasn't out of the woods with all the bad shit I had going on in my life, but when you look at it, everything I lost was taken from me in Virginia. So as far as I'm concerned, leaving here feels like I woke up from a bad dream. What I need to focus on now is this bundle of joy I have inside of me. I've got to make sure I protect him or her at all cost. I have to do this for Sean and me. And when he or she comes into his world, I am going to make sure that they know that their father was a good man and that he protected me just like I'm protecting them. We will have moments where I will share stories about Sean. I may eliminate the part where I was in Witness Protection. But I will say that their father and I were very much in love and talk about the little things like when we ate breakfast together. Or how we'd talk for hours before bedtime. And how I'd laugh at all his jokes. Whatever I needed to say to paint the picture of how great their father was, I'm going to do it. And in Sean's case, it won't be hard to do.

Driving out of the Hampton Bridge-Tunnel, a Virginia State Trooper came out of nowhere and started driving behind me. I damn near panicked as I watched the cop follow me through the rearview mirror. "Oh, my God! He knows who I am. I know he's gonna pull me over at any given minute." I uttered in a whisper like I was preventing someone else from hearing me; that's how paranoid I had become. Two minutes had gone by, and the state trooper hadn't pulled me over nor had he gone around me. I was becoming a nervous wreck thinking about the different scenarios that are probably going to transpire after this guy takes me down. The one scenario that stuck out in my mind was Chad Miller; the fucking rapist had been freed by someone close to him. And that he's probably in the hospital getting his 2nd or 3rd-degree burns treated. It won't surprise me if he's already talked to the cops and gave them precise details about our encounter. I can only hope that I don't get charged for attempted murder. I mean, that bastard did try to rape me. He even tried to kill me. So, I had to take matters in my own hands. It was either him or me, and I chose the latter.

Five more minutes passed, and the state trooper still hadn't pulled me over, and it was driving me fucking crazy. I wanted to pull over and ask him what his problem was, but I knew that would've been a stupid idea, so I continued to drive the speed limit and pray that he eventually leaves me alone.

Finally, after driving for six minutes on I-64, the state trooper made a detour and took Exit 231. I was overjoyed. But I did wonder if he was running the license plates or just trying to scare me into breaking a traffic law. Cops do that all the time. I'm just fortunate that I came out on top of my situation. All I need to do now is make it to Maryland in one peace, so I can see my man laid to rest. After I'm done with that, I'm gonna disappear forever.

****

Immediately after I merged onto Highway I-95 North, I led my head back and started rehearsing what I was going to say to Mrs. Ester when I come to face with her again. One part of me wanted to call her and give her the heads up that I was en route to her house, but I feared that the possibility that the FEDS could have contacted her and told her of my escape. There's also a chance that they could be watching her house to see if I'd show up because they know how badly I wanted to go to Sean's funeral. Either way, I knew it would be my best bet not to call her. The wisest thing I could do was just to pop up unexpectedly. Convince her to help me go to Sean's funeral without anyone knowing I was there. I knew this would be a hard task, but I also knew that it wasn't impossible. That alone gave me the energy to move forward with this plan.

I got chills when I saw the billboard advertising Potomac Mills Mall. It was the biggest mall in America. I wanted to get off on the exit and make a pit stop at this mall because I needed clothes badly, but I was still on Virginia's soil, so I pressed on up Highway I-95 North.

Another 25 minutes into my travels to Maryland, I crossed Virginia and DC state line, and I felt liberated. I felt untouchable. And I felt like I could go and do whatever I wanted. I was finally in control of me. And that's the way I intend to keep it.

I finally stopped off at a corner market in the Southeast section of DC and picked up a burner cell phone, a bag of chips, and a bottle of Sprite. A couple of bystanders looked like they were on the verge of robbing me, but I believe they spared me because I acknowledged them and said what's up. I've always heard that niggas from DC are crazy as hell. The gang violence here was more populated and dangerous than the rough areas of Norfolk, and that's why I'm treading lightly while I'm in their hood.

I wasted little time getting back into the car and hauling ass off these people's territory. But when I saw a Springfield Suites hotel three miles away, I stopped and found a place to hide the car next to the city dumpster. After I backed the car up into the space, I turned off the ignition and began to figure out my next plan. Getting the burner cell phone to work was first on my list. Needing to figure out who I could use to get my hotel room in their name was next on my list. And then after I get that done, finding a spot to buy some clothes would be the last and final thing.

After I activated the burner cell phone, I tested the first call by calling the check cashing place next to the hotel. Their phone number was advertised on their digital banner. "Hello, thanks for calling Ace Check Cashing, how can I help you?" A guy with a foreign accent said.

"I'm sorry I have the wrong number," I replied and then I ended the call.

Holding the phone in my hand, I got the urge to call Mrs. Ester at the number she gave me. But after I pulled the number from my pocket, I froze solid. Anxiety crept back into my heart and caused me to think of all the bad things that would happen if I gave this lady a call. All kinds of doubt plagued me. The what-ifs consumed me. This whole trip up here was beginning to seem like a bad idea. Was I really trying to get caught knowing that the FEDS are going to keep an eye out for me? But then the daredevil inside of me convinced me to be the rebel that I am and keep this train going.

The burner phone took a long time to connect after I dialed Mrs. Ester number. Her line didn't ring until I was getting ready to hang up. All I heard was dead air and then a voice saying, "Hello." I couldn't believe it, but I froze again. My mouth wouldn't move, nor would my hand move. I held the phone to my ear and didn't utter one word. She said hello four times and then she hung up. After the line went dead, I took the phone away from my ear and dropped it in the cupholder. I stared out at the sky and watched two airplanes soar across the sky, but they were going in different directions. That's how I needed to look at my life. Even though I'm going on a different journey, I still need to get up the gumption to take off. If I don't, then I'm going to stay in the slump I'm in and end back up in the hands of the FEDS. Or worse, the niggas that's out here looking for me so they can end my life.

CHAPTER TWELVE

Whitney

"Who was that?" I asked my mother after she answered her phone and then ended it.

She placed her cell phone down on the coffee table in the living room. "I don't know. I said hello, like three to four times." She said, seeming annoyed.

"It probably was Uncle Henry and Aunt Nancy. You know he doesn't really know how to use a cell phone." I joked. And before my mother could comment, the doorbell rang. "That's probably them right there." I continued and got up from the sofa to answer the front door.

"Is it them?" My mother asked me as soon as I took a look through the peephole on the front door.

"Yep, that's them," I announced, and then I opened the front door.

My mother's face lit up when she saw my Uncle Henry and his wife; Aunt Nancy walked into the house. She stood up from the couch and walked mid-floor to greet them. I hugged my Aunt Nancy first, and then I hugged my uncle. After my mother hugged them; she raced off towards the kitchen. "What do you guys want to drink?" She asked them.

"I'm fine." Aunt Nancy said as she took a seat on the sofa and placed her handbag on the floor beside her feet.

"You know I only drink beer." My uncle replied after he sat down next to his wife.

"Henry, you know it's too early to be drinking beer." Aunt Nancy protested.

"Oh, leave him alone. Let him unwind." My mother chimed in as she handed Uncle Henry a bottle of Corona.

"You know I only drink Heineken." He commented after he took the bottle of beer from my mother's hand.

"You'll drink whatever is in that refrigerator." My mother told him and then she took a seat on the love seat across from them.

"Where is your boyfriend, Whitney?" My Aunt Nancy asked me.

"He just stepped out to run a couple of errands," I told her.

"When are y'all two gonna get married? When me and your mother's parents were living, they didn't allow us shacking up." My uncle pointed out.

"Mind your business, Henry. Worry about nursing that beer in your hand." Aunt Nancy scolded him.

"Oh, hush woman. That's my niece. She knows that I'm

only pulling her leg. I helped raise her and her brother like they were mine." He said, and then he looked at the picture of Sean after he graduated from the FBI training academy.

"He was proud of himself that day." I pointed out looking at Sean dressed in a dark blue, two-piece suit, white button-down shirt, and tie, shaking the FBI Director's left hand while the director is handing him his degree with the right hand. That was a really nice day.

"And so was I." My mother interjected.

"It still feels unreal," I added.

"I feel the same way." My mother said.

"Did they give you guys a date for the memorial service?" Aunt Nancy wondered aloud.

"They said I should be hearing from someone no later than tomorrow." My mother replied.

"Are you gonna have the repass here?" Aunt Nancy's questions continued.

"Yeah, I'm gonna get it catered." My mother added.

"Who's all coming?" My uncle chimed back in.

"Just a family and a few of Sean's friends." My mother continued.

"Did you tell Uncle Henry and Aunt Nancy about Lynise?" I blurted out.

Uncle Henry and Aunt Nance both looked at my mother. "Who is that?" Aunt Nancy asked the question first.

"That's the young lady that Sean jumped in the line of fire for, right?" He guessed.

"Yep, that would be her." I pointed out.

"What about her?" Aunt Nancy pressed the issue.

"She's supposed to be pregnant by Sean," I said and got the reaction I was shooting for. Both my uncle and his wife's mouth dropped when I mentioned that Lynise was pregnant. Aunt Nancy looked more shocked that my uncle.

"How do you know she's pregnant?" She questioned me.

"Because when we went to visit her in her hospital room, one of the Physician assistants came in told everyone standing in the room with her that she was pregnant," I explained.

"So, did the Physician assistant also say that it was Sean's baby she was carrying?" Uncle Henry asked.

"My sentiments exactly, Uncle Henry," I replied. It felt good to have someone see things from my perspective, especially about the situation concerning Lynise and that unborn child.

"Listen, Henry; I've been knowing about this girl for about 6-months now. I remember the day he called me and told me that he was in love with her. Now I questioned him about his involvement with her because she was in the witness protection program. But you can't tell a grown-up who to love. And from what I hear, she's been with him the entire time, so I have no reason to question whether or not she's pregnant by Sean."

"She wasn't with Sean the entire time, mom. Remember she ran away from the safe house and ended up getting kidnapped by a taxi driver that was a serial killer." I said.

"Yes, be she was only with him for a week or two." My mother replied.

"Well, if that's the correct time-table, then it sure sounds like it's Sean's baby." Aunt Nancy chimed back in.

"So, where is she now?" Uncle Henry wanted to know.

"No one knows." I blurted out.

"What do you mean, no one knows?" His questions continued.

"One of Sean's agent buddies called mom and told her that she escaped from the hospital yesterday," I stated.

"Sounds like she doesn't like to stay in one place very long." Aunt Nancy commented.

"I said the same thing," I added.

"Is she coming to the memorial service?" Uncle Henry asked.

"She wanted to, but because she's under witness protection, it's prohibited by the bureau." My mother declared.

"Well, shouldn't they make an exception because she's pregnant?" Aunt Nancy indicated.

"See that's the thing, not everyone in the bureau knows. When Whitney and I went back to our hotel, a couple of FBI agents stopped by and told us that they were sent there to post up outside our room just in case Lynise showed up because she may be armed and dangerous. So, I told them both that she couldn't possibly be that dangerous when she two months pregnant. And they both looked at me like I was crazy. Come to find out; they didn't get the memo." My mother stated.

"Sounds like someone dropped the ball." Uncle Henry commented.

"It sure does." Aunt Nancy agreed.

My mother, Uncle Henry and Aunt Nancy talked about Lynise for at least another ten minutes, and from there, they started talking about Sean again and then someone how started reminiscing around my dad. By that time, I had gotten up and went into my bedroom. Getting some alone time was needed, so that's exactly what I did.

CHAPTER THIRTEEN

Lynise

According to the clock on the dashboard of this Honda, I sat out here in this parking lot of the hotel and waited for someone to mosey along so I could get them to get me a room in their name. Thank God for the homeless Vietnam Veteran hanging out around the hotel looking for things to salvage from this dumpster that I was parked beside. When I saw him coming my way, I knew he would be the perfect person to do me a favor for a favor. He was a hippy looking white man, that seemed to be in his late 60's. As soon as I made him the offer to register the room in his name, he couldn't refuse it. Once I had the magnetic key card in my hand, I handed him $50, and he went on his merry way.

The moment I entered the room, I took off my clothes and got in the shower. The hot water felt so good against my skin. It made me feel a sense of calmness. I also felt relaxed and carefree. For that moment, it felt like I was on Cloud 9. What an amazing feeling that was. I just wished that I felt like this all the time, especially with all the chaos I had in my life. I'll figure it out much sooner than later, I hope.

After I got out of the shower, I dried off with one of the big white towels, and then I laid back on the bed buck naked. It was just me, the blanket, and the bedsheets. I went from Cloud 9 to heaven in a matter of twenty-seconds flat.

Now while I was enjoying the comforts of this bed, I heard a knock on the door. The shit scared the hell out of me. "Fuck! Who the hell can't that be?" I whispered underneath my breath as I willed myself up on my feet. On my way to the door, the person knocked two more times. I didn't know what to do, so I stopped in my tracks. "Who is it?" I got up the nerve to say.

"It's housekeeping. I think I left my keys in there." A woman said.

"Hold on, let me check," I told her and then I scanned the room. There was no keys insight. So, I looked in the bathroom, and I didn't see a set of keys in there either. "I'm sorry, but I don't see any keys in here," I assured her.

"Could I come in and check. Because I can't find them anywhere else." She begged me.

I let out a long sigh. "Hold up, wait a minute. Let me put on something." I replied, and then I grabbed one of the bathrobes that were hanging up in the closet by the door and slipped it on. I opened the door right after I tied the belt around me.

Standing there was this short, Hispanic woman that

117

looked to be in her late twenties dressed in her housekeeping uniform. "I am so sorry for bothering you. But I can't seem to find my keys anywhere. And if I don't find them, I could get in big trouble." She explained.

"I didn't see them, but you're welcome to come in and check for yourself." I insisted.

"Thank you so much." She said and then she walked into the room. I stood at the door and watched her as she combed through the room for her keys and after she realized that they weren't here, she apologized for bothering me and then she left. "Don't mention it," I told her then I closed the door behind her.

Not too much longer after the housekeeper left, I threw my clothes back on and left my room to make a store run. I needed to pick up a few things like toiletries, under panties, bras, and a few outfits so I can have clothes to change in and out of. My first stop was Kmart. Then I went to Forever 21. While there, I picked up a few shirts and pants. I even picked out a black dress and a pair of black sunshades to wear to Sean's funeral. I couldn't find a hat at this store, so I found a boutique not too far away and purchased a black hat. After finding everything I needed for the funeral, I stopped at Burger King's drive-thru and ordered a Whopper with cheese meal and a chocolate milkshake. Immediately after the cashier handed me my food, I sped off and headed into the direction of my hotel.

****

I had plans to go in my room, eat my food, watch a little television and relax for the rest of the night but those plans derailed when I opened my hotel room door and saw the fucking homeless man lying on one of the double beds. This cracker scared the shit out of me. He was literally lying on his back with his hands behind his head, watching the local news. "What the fuck are you doing in here?" I yelled at him. I could tell that he had taken a shower too because his long straggly hair was wet and stingy looking.

He sat up on the bed. "What do you mean, why am I in here? This room is in my name." He replied casually like he hadn't done anything wrong.

"I paid you to put this room in your name. That's it." I roared. I was sickened by the mere sight of him. I was even grossed out when I saw his backpacks and old shopping bags with his belongings in them lined up against the wall by the door. The smell was becoming unbearable.

"I'm sorry, but I didn't hear you say that." He replied.

"That's because you probably had a ton of wax in your ear." I snapped.

"You don't have to yell at me, little lady." He protested as he slid towards the edge of the bed.

"I can do what I want to do. Now you've got to leave."

"And go where?"

"Where you were before I met you."

"No way, I can't go back there and give all of this up." He said as if he was living in a fantasy world. I mean this man was really off his rocker. You must be crazy for real if she thought that I asked him to put this room in his name so he and I could sleep in here together.

"Listen, sir, or whatever your name is…"

"It's Clifford. But a lot of people call me Cliff." He interjected.

"Do you think I care about what people call you! I want you to leave this room right now!" I roared. I was coming undone with this game this old ass man was playing with me. Now I'm thinking that this whole plan to get him to get my room in his name backfired on me. So, what was I going to do now?

"You might wanna bring down your tone before one of the other guests call the front desk on you." He warned me.

"You know what? Fuck you! You fucking piece of shit! You can keep this room! And I hope when you go to sleep tonight, that you don't wake up in the morning!" I yelled, and then I turned around and walked out of the room.

Furious because that man just played me, I stormed towards the elevator, hopped on and then I took it to the first-floor lobby. My first thought was to leave the hotel, but I was too tired, and I wanted some rest, so I took a chance and got the hotel room in my name this time. All I could do was hope and pray that the FEDS don't creep up on me tonight after I fall asleep.

The night hotel clerk was a young black woman wearing an old, red lace-front wig that was pre-occupied by her cell phone. I knew she was on Instagram when I heard a guy making a joke, and she burst into laughter. She was definitely into social media. "How can I help you?" She looked up from her phone and asked.

"I wanna get a room for the night," I replied.

"Hey, wait, weren't you with that white guy? I saw him hand you a key card earlier when y'all were outside." She questioned me.

"Well, I wasn't actually with him. I got him to get me a room because I lost my ID and I needed to get a room because I was tired and wanted to get some sleep."

"Oh, so that's why he came to me and got a spare key. He told me that he gave you both keys by mistake and that you left the hotel and he doesn't know when you're coming back."

"That sneaky motherfucker! Do you know that that bastard was laying on the bed watching TV and chilling when I walked in the room." I said and gritted my teeth.

The hotel clerk chuckled. "Don't worry; I'll hook you up. Just give me forty dollars, and I'll give you a room key. But you're going to have to check out by 9:00 because that's when my boss gets here. Okay?"

"Okay," I replied and slid her forty dollars across the counter. She slid a key card across the counter to me a couple of sections later. "I really and truly appreciate this," I told her.

"Don't sweat. Just leave your room before 9:00."

"What's my room number?" I asked her while I was walking away.

"You're on the same floor as before. And I had to put you in the room next to the one you were already in. Room 218."

"That's fine. All I care about is getting some sleep. So,

thank you again." I said, and then I headed back to the elevator. I had a smile on my face that was as big as the moon outside. I was so happy that that young girl looked out for me. I swear, things could've gone south if I had stayed in the room with that man. I would've killed him, or he would've killed me.

****

The second I walked into my new room, I took a deep breath and exhaled. The air was cool, and it was clean. I couldn't get in the bed quick enough. So, after I dropped all my bags on the floor. I got undressed, and then I climbed onto the bed.

There wasn't anything on television that I wanted to watch, so I turned the volume of the TV, turned off all the lights in my room and then I laid down. I was so tired and sleepy and knew that in a few minutes the TV would be watching me instead of me watching it.

I realized that I had dozed off and fell asleep when I heard a thumping noise. Boom! I was scared out of my sleep. I sat up in the bed and sat still. "I don't know where she's at?" I heard a voice say, the words were half-muffled. Then I heard a thud sound as the wall shook. "I told you I don't know." The same voice said, and that's when I realized that what I was hearing was coming from my old room, and I was immediately consumed with fear. What the hell was going on in that room? What was happening to the Vietnam Vet guy? Was someone in there harming him? I needed some fucking answers, but how was I going to get it?

I slid out of bed, tiptoed to the door and peered through the peephole. I figured that whatever was going on next door, the person causing it will have to come out of the room and walked by my door. So, I stood there quietly and held my breath for fear of being heard from the other side of the door. I stood there, heart racing at an uncontrollable speed, wondering if that white man had just gotten hurt. I also wondered was he talking about me when he uttered the words, I don't know where she is. And if he was, then who was he telling that too?

While I thought of every unfortunate possibility, two tall figures walked by my door. It frightened me when I realized that those images looked like men. Once again, fear and anxiety almost paralyzed me. I couldn't see their faces, but I knew that they were black men. Now finding out who those men were, or if they had just come out of that hotel room was not on my to-do list tonight. What I decided to do was climb back into my bed and pray that everything was okay next door.

CHAPTER FOURTEEN
Whitney

The following morning at about 9:30, my mother walks in the kitchen with an announcement while Jeff and I were sitting at the island in the kitchen, talking and drinking coffee. "Well, I just got off the phone with the funeral coordinator and Sean's memorial service is set for Thursday."

"That's three days from now. Don't you think that that's too soon?" I spoke up. In my mind, it felt like my brother's homegoing is going to be rushed and not well-thought-out.

"Well, I'm the one that chose that date. They gave me three options, and I came up with that one." My mother insisted.

"You know that Aunt Daisy and her side of the family may not be able to come because it's such a short notice," I added.

"Well, if they can't come then so be it. Sean is not her son, anyway." My mother replied, sarcastically.

Jeff thought her snide remark was hilarious and chuckled. "I guess my future mother-in-law has just spoken." He commented.

I gave him the evil eye, and he stopped laughing.

"Has his body even made it here yet?" I wondered aloud.

"The woman I spoke to said that it would arrive later today. And tomorrow, they will start dressing him up. The following day we can visit his body at the memorial chapel in Arlington, Virginia. And then the funeral will take place the day after."

Jeff took a sip of his coffee, and then he said, "That guy is going to truly be missed."

"Tell me about it," I commented, and then I took a sip of my coffee too. "Mama, have you figured out what you're going to wear?" I continued.

"I have a ton of black dresses in my closet from attending other family member's funerals so I will choose between one of them."

"Has the FBI found Sean's baby mama, yet?" Jeff blurted out.

Hearing him say the words, baby mama struck a nerve inside of me. I turned around and gave him the evilest facial expression that I could muster up. He threw his hands up like he was waving a white flag. "I'm sorry, but I forgot her name." He confessed.

"Her name is Lynise, Jeff. Lynise." I said sarcastically.

"My bad!" He added.

"Well, I haven't heard anything. So, I'm assuming she's still out there somewhere. I can only hope that she's not in danger." My mother expressed.

"Remember she's from the hood. So, she's fine."

"Honey, didn't I raise you and your brother not to stereotype?" My mother chimed back in.

I sucked my teeth. "Look, mommy, all I'm saying is that she's a tough cookie. She's been through it all. Shootouts! Kidnapping! You name it…."

"Just give it a rest." My mother replied, and then she turned around and walked back out of the kitchen.

"Where are you going?" I asked her while her back was facing me.

"I'm gonna go and take a shower so I can get dressed and go out."

"Where are you going?"

"To your brother's apartment. I need to get a suit from his closet and drop it off to the funeral coordinator." She told me and then she disappeared around the corner.

"That went well," Jeff commented.

"Don't you think that you'd talked enough this morning?" I stated sarcastically. Whether he knew it or not, he was starting to get on my nerves and the morning just started.

"I guess that's my cue." He continued, and then he stood up from the island.

CHAPTER FIFTEEN

Lynise

I woke up to another knock on my door, and when I looked at the time, I shot up from the bed. "Oh, my God! It's 10:00. I know it's the hotel manager." I panicked.

I stood up on my feet and tiptoed back to the door. I stopped in my tracks when the knocking continued. "It's Metro Police. Is anyone in there?" I heard a male's voice boom.

I instantly became paralyzed all over again. I knew that they were there for me. But how? Had my face been plastered all over TV and the night clerk saw it? Did she really rat me out? I was sick on my stomach because I knew I was caught. There was no way I was going to get out of this jam.

Boom! Boom! Boom! "Metro police, is anyone in there?" I heard another male's voice announce out in the hallway. But he wasn't knocking on my door. It sounded like he was knocking on the door in front of mine. "What is going on?" I uttered softly. I continued to stand there and waited to see what I would hear next.

"Hi there, sir, my name is Detective Allen, and I'm going around to everyone's room on this floor to find out if anyone heard any kind of commotion going on in that room across from you." I heard him say.

"No, I'm afraid not. I didn't hear anything. What happened if you don't mind me asking?" The hotel guest asked.

"There was a homicide, and unfortunately, the guest that was staying in that room was murdered." I heard the cop say.

"Metro Police, is there someone in there?" I heard another voice yell. The knocking and voice was a little faint, so I knew the cop had to be knocking on someone's door about three to four doors down.

"Oh, my God! So, the guy next door got killed." I said, my words barely audible while trying to wrap my mind around what the cop just said to the guest across from me and what I heard last night. "I fucking knew it. I knew someone was doing something to that man last night." I continued while my words came out in a whisper. Then it hit me, that when I heard the older man was saying, that *he didn't know where she was*, he was talking about me. But who the fuck was asking him those questions?

My heart began at a rapid speed while trying to piece together all the events that happened from the time I went into that room and when I left. Okay, so after I went into the room, I took a shower, I laid down on the bed, the housekeeper knocked on the door, I let her in and then she left. After that, I got dressed, left the room, went to the store, got something to eat and then I came back to the hotel. When I walked back into the room, the old man was lying on one of the beds with his hands placed behind his hands. I cursed him out and then I left the room. After I left, I got my own room, crawled in the bed, and fell asleep after that. But not too long after that, I woke up from my sleep when I heard bumping noises and the guy telling someone that he didn't know where the girl was. And that girl had to be me.

Instantly crippled by the thought that if I was in that room last night, I would've gotten murdered instead of that man. But who it could've been? Who knew I was at this hotel? And that's when it hit me….. "Oh, my God! The fucking housekeeper set me up. That fucking bitch!" I hissed. "She's the reason that that man is dead."

Terrified that that hit that was intended to happen to me, I got dressed and grabbed my things. Once I had all my stuff in hand, I waited patiently for the commotion surrounding the murder of the old man to die down. I thought that I could've left sooner but I couldn't. The hallway became crawling with cops and a forensics team. Thank God that the girl from the front desk didn't list me as a guest, because there was no question in my mind that those cops would've gotten a key to come into my room after I purposely didn't answer after they knocked on my door.

I paced the floor and watched the clock on the nightstand, I until I heard the last coroner announce to his collogue that he was ready to take the body downstairs to the van. "Are the detectives coming back?" I heard one of the guys say.

"No, they aren't coming back. So, we can lock up." I heard another voice reply.

"Let's do it." The other voice chimed back in.

I heard a little bit of rustling, and then I heard the door close. After I saw the guys walk by my door while looking out of the peephole, I grabbed my things and waited patiently. I actually waited for three minutes, and then I opened my door quietly. I peered around the corner of the door, and when I saw that the coast was clear, I darted out of the door and raced for the stairway. It only took me a matter of eight seconds to get down to the first floor, and when I arrived at the door that led to the lobby, I took a deep breath, and then I exhaled. "Come on, Lynise; you can do it, girl. Just take your time." I said, giving myself a pep talk.

Once I got up the nerve, I opened the door as quietly as I could and carefully looked around into the lobby. There were two people standing there. Unfortunately for me, one of them happened to be a white man dressed brown khakis, a black t-shirt, and a bullet-proof vest, the other person, was the young girl from the night before. They were doing an extensive amount of talking so it wouldn't shock me if she spilled the beans on me and my roll in the room situation. Not only that, she knew that I was upset so I could've easily killed that homeless guy myself. Without further hesitation, I looked in the opposite direction of the lobby and noticed that I could slide out of the side door of the hotel without the cop or the night clerk from seeing me. The only problem was that I had to step in the hallway and close the door softly to keep from it clicking. So, I pulled back on the door wide enough so that I could fit my body in the opening. Then I moved my body to the entryway, but not so far that I could be seen. I rested my back against the door and waited for the perfect timing to ease my way into the hallway without making any noise.

"If you can think of anything else, call me at this number. If I don't answer, then leave me a message." I heard the cop say. Still standing in the doorway, another wave of fear and anxiety went through me because I knew the cop was leaving, I just don't know which door he's leaving out of. So, I pushed the stairwell door back with my body, and then I jumped behind it and started pushing it close before he could detect that someone was there. But it didn't work. I struggled to close the door in a fast manner because it was too heavy. Thank God the cop didn't use the side exit door to leave the hotel. If he had, I would've been caught.

I waited another couple of minutes before I made my way into the hallway. I had to make sure that no one was around. So, as I power walk down the hall towards the side door, I prayed that there were no more cops lingering around outside. I had already stayed at the hotel longer than I had expected. I can only hope that I hadn't missed out on anything. If I had, then I'm going to be pissed.

The moment I pushed the side door open, I looked

into the parking lot for my car. I didn't see it at first, and I became alarmed. I rushed outside and realized that the bush in front of me was blocking my view, so I walked further to the curb and stumbled into the housekeeping woman from the day before. She was dressed in her uniform, standing behind the bush smoking a cigarette. She looked at me like she was a deer in headlights. She stood there and didn't say a word. I guess she was waiting for me to say something first. I began approaching her, and she started walking backwards. "Bitch, you tried to set me up yesterday. Coming to my room, talking about you lost your keys, knowing damn well you didn't lose shit." I roared.

"That's not true. I did lose my keys." She said, sticking to her story.

"Stop lying and tell me who told you to come to my room yesterday?" I growled and grabbed her around her throat. She dropped her cigarette and stumbled backwards, but I kept my hold around her neck. She started choking and begging me to let her go.

"Let me go, and I'll tell you." She pleaded.

I released my hand from her neck. She coughed a couple of times, and then she cleared her throat. "I don't know who they were. They just showed up on my floor and showed me a picture of you and told me to check every room until I find out which room you were in." She cried.

"How did they look?" I wanted to know.

"They were tall, black guys. They looked really mean in the face."

"Do you know what you did was wrong on all levels? You're the reason that man got killed last night, right?" I told her while gritting my teeth at her.

"They said that they weren't going to harm anybody. They promised me." She began to sob loudly.

"Look, it's too late for all the tears. That man died because you put him in harm's way." I began to say, "Tell me how much money they paid you because I know they gave you something." I continued and gave her the side-eye.

"One hundred dollars." She replied.

"One hundred dollars?! That's it?" I questioned her. But I was more shocked than ever.

"Yes, that's all they gave me." She assured me while wiping the tears from her face.

"So, you let a man get killed, and all you got was one hundred dollars?!" I responded sarcastically.

"They said that they were looking for you." She corrected me.

"Oh, so because they were looking for me, one hundred dollars was still appropriate?" I asked her.

"No... they said that they weren't here to harm anyone."

"Well, they lied, and now the cops are all over this place looking for me because I was the last person that white guy talked to."

"Please don't report me to my supervisor." She begged me.

"Are you fucking serious right now?! I can't believe that

you're more concerned about me going to your supervisor than the fact that someone got murdered." I spat. I swear, I wanted to punch her in her fucking face.

"I'm sorry, but I don't make much money so I can't lose my job." She explained.

"Fuck your job! You need to be more concerned about the cops than your job. Because if you hadn't told those guys that I was in that room, then we wouldn't be having this conversation. I mean, do you realize that I could be dead right now if I hadn't left that room last night?" I snapped as I leaned in towards her.

"I told you I was sorry."

"Bitch, kiss my ass!" I roared, and then I backed away from her. "You better do everything in your power to convince the cops that I didn't kill that man. And if you don't, then I'm gonna tell them that you set the whole thing up." I threatened her, and then I walked away.

When I looked out at the parking lot, I saw the car parked about 200 yards away from where I was standing, so I looked both ways to make sure no cops were around, and when I figured that the coast was clear, I made a run for my car. It took me less than one minute to open the door, throw my things onto the front seat, start up the ignition, and get out of there. And once I was on the road, I looked through the rearview mirror one time to make sure that I wasn't being followed. And when I felt like I was in the clear, I headed towards Highway 495 North. This highway would take me to Mrs. Ester's home, and I need to get there now more than ever.

CHAPTER SIXTEEN

Whitney

My family and friends really showed my mother, and I love by coming to our home and paying their respects at our time of loss. I swear Sean would be so proud of us all. Now as the night winded down, everyone from my cousins to my aunts and my uncles started trickling out of the house one by one. Every time two people walked out, two more walked out. It didn't matter because my mother and I were extremely tired of playing host. All she and I wanted to do was get off our feet and relax.

While she was saying goodbye to our next-door neighbors, her cell phone started ringing. I picked it up from the coffee table and answered it. "Hello," I said. But I got dead air. "Hello," I said again. But once again I got dead air. So, I took the phone from my ear and looked at the caller ID. There was no phone number displayed. "Hello, is somebody there?" I asked after putting the phone back up to my ear. But for the last time I still only got dead air, and that's when I disconnected the call.

"Did somebody just prank call you?" Jeff walked up on me and asked.

"Probably. Who knows," I replied.

"Where did you just come from?" I asked him after I placed my mother's cell phone back on the coffee table.

"From the back patio. I had to pull the trash bends to the curb. Trash day is tomorrow." He continued as he took a seat next to me on the sofa.

"Did you get a piece of that cake that Aunt Nancy baked?"

"Nah, not yet. But I heard it was good."

"Yeah, it was. I eat two slices and put me another slice of it for later."

"Do you and mama decide who was doing the eulogy?" He wanted to know.

"Mama said she wants her pastor to do it, so there you go."

"You sound like you're mad about it."

"No, I'm good. I just thought that it should've been someone in our family. But I'm gonna respect her wishes and be done with it."

"Did the funeral coordinator say how long the service is going to be?"

Before I could answer his question, my mother's cell phone started ringing again. I picked it back up and answered it on the second ring. "Hello," I said. But got dead air. "Hello," I spoke into the phone again and got no answer. "Look, I don't know who this is on this phone, but you need to stop wasting people's time." I snapped, and then I disconnected the call.

After I sat my mother's phone back down on the coffee table, Jeff said, "I betcha' that's Lynise calling your mother."

Caught off guard by his assumption, I sat there and mulled over the possibility that he could be right. "You know what, you're probably right." I agreed.

"What are you right about Jeff?" I mother interjected as she had taken a seat on the other sofa.

"Your phone keeps ringing, and every time I answer it, no one says anything. So, Jeff thinks that it's Lynise calling but won't say anything because I'm not the one she wants to talk to." I explained.

"Hand me my phone." My mother instructed me as she held her hand out for it. After she took it from me, she pushed it down into her front pants pocket.

"Are you gonna talk to her if that's, in fact, her calling your phone?" I wanted to know.

"Of course, I am."

"Well, I hope you tell her that there's an APB out on her."

"She probably wants to come to the memorial service." Jeff chimed in.

"Yeah, she's been saying it all the long," I added.

"Well, if it's her calling, I will tell her that the FBI is looking for her and that she should turn herself in. It will kill me if something happens to her while she's carrying that baby." My mother pointed out.

"Can we just find out if she's carrying Sean's baby before we start carrying?" I commented sarcastically. My mother is driving me crazy about this baby situation. We need to focus on getting my brother buried, and then after that, we can take care of a paternity test.

"Look, I'm tired, and I'm gonna go and retire to my room now." She stated and then she got up and left the room.

"Love you, mama," I said aloud.

"Yeah, mama, I love you too," Jeff announced.

"Yeah, yeah, yeah, I love you both too," She responded as she continued walking in the direction of her bedroom.

CHAPTER SEVENTEEN

Lynise

"If that bitch keeps answering her mother's phone, I am going to curse her out. I mean, give your mother her cell phone and stop answering it. I am not calling you so get a fucking life already and go crawl into your man's arms. Ugh!" I roared while driving north on Highway 395. I had to get out of D.C. before another incident happened that I can't take back.

I drove to Bethesda, Maryland, and found a cozy spot in a parking garage since I couldn't risk getting caught. I was sure someone was on my tail. I just didn't know who.

Now while I was hiding out in this garage, I realized that it'd been an hour since I tried to call Mrs. Ester's cell phone back so I redialed her number and hoped that Whitney wouldn't answer it this time.

This time the call went straight through and what do you know, Mrs. Ester answered it on the second ring. "Hello," she said. When I heard her voice, it was like music to my ears.

"Hi, Mrs. Ester," I replied cheerfully.

"Yes, this is she."

"Hi, this is Lynise."

"Hi Lynise, how are you?"

"Not too good. Got a lot of stuff going on."

"You know the FBI is looking for you?"

"Yes, ma'am, I know."

"Are you safe?"

"Yes, ma'am."

"Well, we bury Sean the day after tomorrow at the Arlington Cemetery."

"What time?" I wondered aloud. I needed details so I could plan accordingly.

"Three o'clock in the evening."

"Will it be an open casket?"

"No, we think it's best to keep the casket closed. We want to remember him as a great son, and loving brother and talk about all the good things he did."

"That's understandable."

"Did you happen to call my cell phone earlier? Because Whitney said, someone called twice but wouldn't say anything."

"Yes, that was me. And I'm sorry about that."

"No need to be sorry. But I do want you to be careful out there because Sean's agent buddies are looking for you. And they suspect that you're coming to the funeral so watch your back."

"I appreciate the heads up. But I already knew that. Those guys are so predictable."

"Regardless if they're unpredictable or not, you gotta be smart about things. You can't run forever."

"I know," I replied and then I let out a long sigh. "I don't know if you know this, but I've had a rough life since I was a small kid. I never felt the love from anyone, and that goes for my mother and father. And the only best friend I had stabbed me in the back. So, you see, I've always had to look out for myself. Trust me, nothing or no one is going to keep me down."

"Sweetheart, anything can happen. So, please be careful."

"Don't worry; I will."

****

It felt good to talk to Mrs. Ester. It also felt good to know that she had my back. I mean, she didn't know me so; therefore, she didn't have to tell me what was going on behind the scenes. That dumb ass daughter of hers was trying my patience. She needs to get out of her feelings and stop blaming me for Sean's death because it wasn't my fault. I want him here as much as she does. But he's not so we've got to lay him to rest and then move on with our lives.

CHAPTER EIGHTEEN
Whitney

"What are you doing?" Jeff asked me after sneaking up behind.

Startled by his unexpected presence, I turned around from my mother bedroom door and slapped his arm. "Don't ever sneak up behind me like that. You scared the shit out of me." I whispered and pushed him out of the way.

I headed down the hallway and into the kitchen. He followed me. "You know it's impolite to eavesdrop on other people's conversations." He made me painfully aware after he entered the kitchen behind me.

"Yes, I do. But I also know that it's impolite to sneak up behind someone and scare the crap out of them too." I pointed out.

"You're shifting the blame." He said. He wasn't let up. He wanted me to own my part in this situation.

"Look, I don't care. I will take the blame. And I'm glad I did it too because I found out that it was Lynise calling mama. When you walked up behind me, mama had just hung up with her."

"What did mama say?"

"Oh, so now you wanna know what was said?" I replied sarcastically.

"I'm just curious is all."

"Well, let's just say that mama told her everything. She told her that the FBI is looking for her. She told her where Sean's memorial service is going to be, and she told her the time."

"Wow! She did tell her everything." Jeff said in a shocked manner.

"I wonder if she's gonna still go to the funeral knowing that the FBI will be waiting for her?"

"The person I saw at the hospital, yes she will. I mean, come on…. She's a fucking renegade. She's escaped from a safe house, kidnappers, and managed to stay alive all while being pregnant." I pointed out.

"She's Bonney without the Clyde." Jeff chuckled.

"So, you think all of this is funny, huh?"

"No, but you gotta give it to homegirl, she's definitely a warrior."

I sucked my teeth. "She's gonna be a locked up warrior after I get through with this."

"Whatcha' gonna do?"

"I'm gonna call the agents that gave me their card. They need to know that she called mama."

"Come on, Whitney, stay out of that."

"I'm not staying out of anything. There are bad men looking for her. The same men that killed my brother, so do you think that I am going to allow her to come around my mother or communicate with her because she thinks that she's carrying my brother's baby? Hell no! Those men that want her will not stop until they kill her. And one day they will track her down and do it. But my mother will not be around when it happens." I stated, and then I left the kitchen.

My cell phone was on the table in the foyer, so I grabbed it, and I grabbed my purse from the hallway closet. Once I had it in my hands, I sifted through the contents until I found the agent's card. "Here you go," I said after pulling the business out. With both things in hand, I sat my purse down on the table in the foyer and headed out the front door. I walked over to my car and proceeded to call the phone number on the card. The phone only rang once and then my call was answered. "This is Special Agent Snow.

"Hi, Agent Snow. My name is Whitney Foster, and you gave me your card at the hotel and told me to call you if I had any information or concerning Lynise." I began to explain.

"Yes, I remember now whatcha' got for me?" He replied. He got straight to the point.

"My mother finally got a call from Lynise."

"Oh really,"

"Yes,"

"Did you hear the conversation?"

"I heard what my mother was saying."

"And what did your mother say?"

"She told her where the memorial services will be and what time it starts. And she also told her that you guys' were looking for her."

"Oh, that's not good." He said sarcastically.

"Well, it may not be good in your eyes, but that's what she told her."

"Did she mention coming to your mother's house?"

"I told you that I only heard my mother's words."

"Well, I appreciate you calling me, now I will handle things on this end."

"Is that it?"

"Yep, that's it. But if she happens to contact your mother again, please don't hesitate to call again." He reminded me.

"Yeah, okay," I said, and then I disconnected the call.

I looked up after I hung up with the agent. And what do you know, Jeff was standing at the front door watching me. I know he's probably mad that I made this phone call to the agent, but I had to do what was right for my mother. And if that includes keeping her out of danger, then so be it.

CHAPTER NINETEEN

Lynise

Today was the day Sean would be laid to rest. After sleeping in the car for two days straight, the aches in my back were starting to take a toll on me. But when I weighed the pros and cons of back pains versus the FEDS storming into a hotel room after a night clerk rats me out, I preferred the backaches.

Like I did the previous day, I went into the bathroom of a restaurant when they first open to bathe because I knew it would be clean. Today was no different. So, after I changed into my clothes for Sean's memorial service, I exited the bathroom and headed back out to my car. On my way to the car, I saw a woman that looked just like me walk by. It was like I was in the twilight zone. I couldn't believe my own eyes. She was carrying a messenger bag across her shoulders and a Walgreens shopping bag in her hands. I stood there and watched her as she walked over to the bus stop and took a seat on the bench. I couldn't believe all the thoughts that I had racing through my mind. But the one that stuck out the most was a plan that I had to execute. I walked over to where she was and introduced myself. "Hi, my name is Lynise, how are you?" I asked her. And when I got a closer look at her, I saw how I would look if I were on drugs. This lady's eyes were sunken in; her lips were severely cracked; she had sores on her face. If you can think about the worse looking dope fiend, this lady was it.

"I'm doing fine, and you?" She replied, her words came out slow.

I took a seat beside her. "What's your name?" My questions continued.

"Pamela,"

"Do you live around here?"

"Yeah, why?" she gave me a suspicious look.

"Nothing really. I'm just making conversation."

"Look I know you want something so tell me what it is."

"What makes you say that?"

"Listen, lady; I am a junkie! And where I come from everybody wants something." She spat. She was getting very frustrated with me.

"Okay, check it out, I want you to pose as you're me."

"Pose as you? What the hell are you talking about?" She replied, becoming more annoyed by the second.

"I need you to go to a funeral and act like you're me," I replied.

"Act like you?" She chuckled. "Girl, we don't look nothing alike."

"Look, I'm gonna dress you in black clothes and give

you sunshades to wear. And you'll look just like me." I pressed her.

"Are you paying me?"

"Yes, I will pay you."

"How much?"

"One hundred dollars."

"One hundred dollars!"

"Yeah," I assured her.

"Well, what's the hold-up. Let's get this party on the road." She said and stood up from the bench.

I escorted Pam to my car, and we were on our merry way. Since she was from this area, she showed me where I could buy her a black dress, high heels, a hat, and dark sunshades. It took us less than thirty minutes to get everything we needed. We stopped by a corner spot and got another burner phone too. Pam was going to need it with the plan I have in mind.

Now while we were in route to her friend's apartment so she could get dress, she decides that she wants to get a couple of pills of dope first because she doesn't want to get ill while attending the funeral.

Knowing firsthand, that junkies will get sick if they don't get their regular fix of heroin, I asked her where she wanted me to go, and then I took her. After I pulled up curbside, I gave her thirty of the one hundred dollars I promised her and then she disappeared on the side of an old abandoned house.

Smiling from ear to ear with three capsules of heroin in hand, Pam was ready to take care of business. "Mine if I sniff this first one?" She asked me.

"I thought you shoot up?"

"I do when I only have one pill of dope. But since I have three, I'll sniff the first one just to keep the edge off when I don't have a needle with me."

"Oh, okay," I said nonchalantly. "Are we going to your friend's house now?" I questioned her.

"Yeah, take a right turn at the next block and then take that road all the way down until you see the light blue house on the left side." She instructed me.

"So, we're going to a light blue house?"

"It's a rooming house. It's about five people that rents the rooms out of it. And my friend's room is in the back of the house." She explained.

As instructed by Pam, I took her route, and within minutes we were directly in front of the rooming house. "Come on; we gotta walk around back." She told me, and I followed.

When we walked into the house, a foul odor of trash permeated the entire downstairs level. I gagged immediately after I breathe it in. "Somebody needs to take that trash out," I complained.

"I don't smell it," Pam commented.

"That's because you're immune to it," I told her while covering my nose.

Pam escorted me to a smile room located only ten feet away from the back door of the house. Her friend wasn't there. Thank God, because the room was no bigger than a closet. And

I'm not talking about a walk-in closet either.

"Wanna sit down?"

"Nah, I'm good. Just hurry up because the funeral is going to be starting soon." I lied. The funeral wasn't starting for another three and a half hours. But I needed those extra hours to get to the cemetery since it's in Arlington, Virginia. Not only that, I knew that I had to get Pam set up. I figured that if I got here there before everyone arrived, I could position her to walk on the scene while the service was going on. Out of respect for Sean's family and friends, the FEDS won't interrupt funeral by trying to take her in custody. I do, however, believe that as soon as the memorial service is over, they're going to come in full force. But the best part of it all is when they take off her sunglasses and find out that she's not me. Oh, my goodness, they're going to be pissed. Their facial expressions are going to be priceless.

****

Pam finally got dressed and climbed into the car with me. We hit the highway 395 South and headed directly towards Arlington, Virginia. Pam slept the entire way there, but as soon as we merged off the exit, I woke her up and told her to get ready. "I'm ready," She said with certainty.

I got off on Exit 7B for Glebe Road, and then I made a right turn Quincy Street. I drove another a half-mile on Quincy Street, and then I finally made a right on Wilson Road. I took the back road in to keep from being spotted. I parked my car behind the storage shed. There was a white guy dressed in landscaping attire packing shovels and other garden tools on a small truck. At first glance, he looked like a federal agent, but when I looked at his body language, I knew that he wasn't. There's a certain way that FBI agents walk. The way they carry themselves and this guy didn't have it. So, I grabbed her by the arm and escorted her out of the car. "There's a lot of people are here. How many funerals does this place having daily?"

"Twenty-five. Maybe thirty." He replied.

"Do you know where Special Agent Foster is supposed to be buried today?" I asked the guy.

"Oh, he's at section 13 off Garfield Drive."

"Is that far from where we are now?"

"Yes, it's on the other side."

"I would pay you if you could take us there."

"There's only room for one person."

"Well, could you take her?"

"Yes, I can do that."

"When he takes you to where the actual funeral is, walk away from it and when I see you walking away, I'm gonna call you with more instructions. Okay?" I whispered in her ear.

"Okay. But when am I gonna get the rest of my money?" She inquired.

"After this is over," I told her.

"Okay," she replied, and then she got into the truck.

"Hey sir, do you have a pair of binoculars I could borrow? I promise I will give them back to you. As a matter of fact, I'll give you twenty more dollars to use them. And when I'm done, you can get them right back." I assured.

He grabbed a pair of binoculars from a metal tool case that was on the back of his truck. And in total, I handed him forty dollars. After he had his money in hand, he got in the truck with Pam. I watched them as they drove away. I looked around the entire cemetery with the binoculars and quickly realized that this place was huge. I have never in my life seen such a massive place. I know it would take hours to walk around it. Thank God that I don't have to.

As soon as the guy dropped Pam off at the area where Sean was scheduled to be buried, she called my burner phone. "So, whatcha' want me to do?" She didn't hesitate to ask.

"Go stand by that group of people but go sit on that stone bench with your back facing them," I instructed her.

Following my instructions to a tee, Pam sat down on the stone bench and had her back facing the crowd a few yards from here. "Since nobody is looking at me, can I take my needle out and get a quick fix?" She asked me.

My first thought was to tell her hell no. But then I remembered that if I tell her no, she's going to do it anyway or leave this place altogether. So, I told her yes. "Please do not let anyone see you using that needle. There are guards all around her, and they will arrest you if you don't be careful."

"Don't worry; I won't get caught." She said.

"Okay," I said, and then I disconnected the call.

CHAPTER TWENTY

Whitney

The drive to the cemetery wasn't that bad. My mother talked to Jeff and me to death the whole way there. "I've been wondering all morning if Lynise is going to try her luck and attend Sean's memorial service," I said aloud, wanting my mother to chime in. I knew she told Lynise that the agents were looking for her. I eavesdropped on her phone call. I just wanted her to admit it.

"I hope she doesn't." Jeff chimed in. I gave him the evil eye because that comment wasn't for him; it was for my mother.

"Why not?" I asked him. I was curious to hear his stupid ass response.

"Because the agents will be there and it could get really ugly. And now wouldn't be a good time to arrest her. She doesn't need that type of drama while she's pregnant." He explained.

"Wake up! Life is just that, drama!" I replied sarcastically.

"I can't argue that," Jeff added and then he fell silent.

"What about you, mama? Think she's gonna come?" I pressed the issue.

"She may... she may not." She commented all while looking out of the passenger side window.

"Have you spoken with her lately?" I wanted to know.
"Yes, I've spoken to her."

"And what did she say?"

"Not much."

"Did you tell her that the agents are looking for her?"

"Yes, she knows."

"Mama, I want you to cut all contact off with her. It's dangerous being around her. Now, I lost Sean; I refuse to lose you too." I gripped. I needed my mother to know that I loved her, and I won't tolerate her putting herself in harm's way behind that crazy ass chick.

"Whitney, I'm a big girl, so therefore I can handle myself."

"Yeah, your son said the same thing, now we're on our way to his funeral." I vented. I needed her to understand that wherever that girl goes, people get killed.

"Come on, Whitney, that's not necessary," Jeff interjected.

"She needs to hear what I'm saying. We've already lost my dad and now, Sean. If I lose mama, just check me into a mental hospital." I commented.

"No one is losing anyone. Now let's just drop this conversation." Jeff concluded, and then he fell silent. I didn't say another word either. The tension in this car was so thick that it could be cut with a knife.

We finally arrived inside of the cemetery and saw a few family members and agent buddies of Sean. After I parked my car, I looked around to see if I saw Lynise standing around in the cut somewhere. But I didn't see her on my radar.

Jeff climbed out of the car and helped my mother out of the front passenger side. Once she was out of the car, Jeff escorted her over to the burial site and I followed them. "Be careful you two, the ground is somewhat damped," I warned them.

"We got it," Jeff assured me.

At our designated site location, my mother and I were greeted by all of Sean's colleagues, family, and friends. Then we were shown to our seats. My mother's pastor started the services, and surprisingly, Jeff stood up and gave the eulogy. After Jeff finished, he passed the torch to me, and I said a few words. I told everyone there that I was Sean's twin sister and how he's going to be missed. I also told them how big of a heart that Sean had. Now when I started talking about the things we used to do to get out of trouble, I saw a woman standing just a few feet away from our site sitting on a stone bench. She wore all black. And she even wore a black hat and black sunglasses. There was no doubt in my mind that that was Lynise. She was sitting there watching as the service ran on.

I looked over and gave two of the agents' nod, letting them know that Lynise was here and that she was right behind us. They caught on and looked over their shoulders. My mother caught on to what I was doing too. She gave me the evil eye, and I pretended that I didn't see it. In my mind, I'm saying, "Let the games begin."

CHAPTER TWENTY-ONE

Lynise

I stood there and watched as Pam sat on the stone bench, looking into the direction of Sean's memorial service. She was playing the part to the tee. But when she nodded her head, I knew the heroin was taking its effects on her. So, in my mind, I'm praying that she doesn't fuck up my plan. I needed her just to sit there and pretend to be me. That's it. "Come on, Pam, let's keep it together," I uttered softly while watching her through the binoculars.

In the middle of watching the service take place, I couldn't shake a tall figure in my peripheral vision. I looked to my right and saw a man dressed in all black sneak up behind, uttered a few words to her and when she turned around, he shot her in the face, point-blank range. She immediately collapsed onto the ground. I stood there in horror because I didn't pay that woman to get killed. I paid her to stand there and pretend like she was me so I could watch Sean's memorial services without any interruptions since Whitney tipped off the FEDS that I was going to be here. But who would've thought that a mad man would go to lengths to kill me at a funeral where there's going to be a dozen of FBI agents swarming this place? "FBI! Get down on your knees!" I heard two agents scream out after one another.

I stood there with my heart aching because a woman disguised as me die. Why the fuck is everybody around me getting fucking killed. She was only supposed to trick the agents into believing that she was me. That's it. Now the poor lady is dead.

"I said, get down!" One of the same agents roared.

The two agents finally got the guy to lay down on his stomach. After they handcuffed him, they pulled him up from the ground, and when he stood up, my heart sunk into the pit of my stomach. I couldn't believe it, but it was Bishop. Bishop in the flesh and he thought that he had just killed me. Mrs. Ester already told me that the FBI would be watching me. So, did they use me as bait to lure Bishop in? Of course, they did. Fucking bastards! In their minds, they were killing two birds with one stone. But guess what? They've got bigger problems now. If they knew that I was going to be here, then why not capture Bishop before he pulled the trigger? I know what. They wanted to get rid of me. I've been a hassle to them, so they need me out of the way. And what an easy way to do it. But they fucked up! And now that woman's blood is on their hands.

Like I planned, I managed to get out of the cemetery

untouched. I guess now I can go on with my life. But then I remembered that I one last mission to finish.

****

I knew that I couldn't leave this place without tying up one last loose end. Paying Jimmy's mother, a visit was a major necessity. I refused to let her breathe another day, especially after what she and her psycho ass son did to me and all those other innocent women they victimized.

I rang the doorbell and disguised my voice after she asked who was at her front door. "Sorry to bother you ma'am, but my car caught a flat tire, and my cell phone just went dead so could I use your phone to call AAA?" I asked respectfully, hoping this would get her to open her door.

"I'm sorry, but it's too late for me to be opening my front door for people I don't know." She replied.

"Fuck!" I said in a whisper. I couldn't afford to let her hear me. "I'm alone. And it won't take long." I continued while crossing my fingers that she would give in and let me into her house.

"No, I'm sorry. But it's too late."

"I'll tell you what, you could bring your phone to the front door and hand it to me while I'm still out here," I suggested. I was pulling tooth and nail now trying to come up with ways for her to open her door for me.

She didn't reply. She went radio silent. "Hello, ma'am, are you still there?" I asked nicely.

"Hold on a minute," she finally said, and then it went radio silent again.

After waiting for what seemed like forever, I finally heard the front door unlocking. And then the cricking sounds of the door opening slowly. A smile ray of light from the hallway of her house peaked through the slightly ajar door, and then a cordless phone appeared with her hand on the other end of it. I couldn't see her face, and she couldn't see mine so I felt like this would be the perfect opportunity to kick her door in. "Take this phone, but you hurry up so I can close my door." She instructed me.

At that very moment, I lunged back and pushed back on the front door with all the strength I had in my upper body. Boom was the sound I heard when the front door pushed back on her wheelchair. Startled, she screamed, "Arrrrrrgg, what are you doing?"

Unfortunately for me, my initial blow didn't get the door open far enough for me to break in, so I lunged back and turned sideways as I charged at it. Boom!

Now this time, I was able to come face to face with this evil old lady. It was dark outside, but there was light in her house, and it shined down on my face. "What do you want with me?" She yelled, the instant she laid eyes on me after dropping the cordless phone on the floor. I had managed to push her wheelchair back a couple of feet away from the door. This gave me plenty of space to walk into her home. I swear, she looked like she had seen a freaking ghost.

After I got within one foot of her, I grabbed that bitch by her throat with my right hand and started applying a lot of pressure to her neck. "What do I want with you?" I started off saying while I gritted my teeth at her. "Did you think that I was going to let you get away with how you and your psychopathic ass son did to me?"

She tried to speak, but her words were barely audible because I was squeezing the life out of her. I honestly didn't want to hear anything she had to say. "Bitch, y'all two damn near sucked the life out of me. So, guess what? You're gonna pay for everything you and your son did to me and all of those other innocent girls." I stated, and I meant every word of it. No other woman will ever have to suffer again because of them. Tonight, she was going to meet her maker.

"Die, bitch!" I uttered, giving her a menacing expression after I applied my left hand to her throat. She tried stopping me by hitting me in my side, but my pressure to her neck was no match for power in the punches she was applying to the stomach area of my body.

I watched her as her face color changed to pink and then purple. Her resistance level decreased too. Seconds later, her body went limp. I stood there and looked at her for a few minutes and wondered where I was going now because I have no one. Everyone from my past is dead. So, wherever life takes me, will I ever find love again? I guess I will soon find out.

Epilogue

Jeff, me and my mother, sat around the living room after we cleared everyone out of the house that came to spend time with us at our repass. We were exhausted, and our faces showed it. But that didn't stop a conversation about Lynise. "I still can't believe that that lady was dead," Jeff spoke first.

"Neither can I." I chimed in. "And she looked so much like Lynise." I continued, staring up into the ceiling.

"That guy Bishop thought so too that's why he shot her in the head," Jeff added.

"He was a big guy." My mother said.

"Yeah, he was," I commented.

"Do you think that Lynise set that whole thing up?" Jeff wanted to know.

"Of course, she did. It was set up to nicely."

"I wonder where she was when the agents rushed that guy, Bishop?" Jeff questions continued.

"She was somewhere near, watching everything as it unfolded,"

I answered him.

"Think we're gonna ever see her again?"

"Only time will tell," I concluded because that was the only answer I could come up with. The agents told my mother and I that that lady we thought was Lynise was a heroin addict. They also told us that she had drugs on her when she O'd. And when Bishop shot her in the head, she was already dead. Now I have to admit that I underestimated Lynise. She was smarter than I thought she was. The only thing now is, will we ever see her again now that the FEDS finally had Bishop in custody? I guess we'll see.

SNEAK PEEK INTO:

Behind Closed Doors

Coming Out January 2020

Kiki Swinson

BEHIND
Closed Doors

Kiki Swinson

Chapter One
My Screwed Up Life

The sun sparkled over the Epstein family's summer home in the Hamptons. The sunlit lawn is why they'd chosen the property. The home was a huge mansion in an exclusive gated community, sat on top of a hill with gorgeous views from every room. The natural sunlight hit the well-manicured lawn like a movie spotlight. Evelyn Epstein stood with her arms folded across her chest, staring out at the massive landscape. She inhaled the fresh scent of the newly cut grass and let out a long-exasperated breath. She had so much on her mind. Evelyn and her family had been coming to the Hamptons from New York City each summer for eighteen years now, and with every passing year, the façade they put on of the perfect little family seemed to crack a little more. She shuddered just thinking about how much things had crumbled. No more picture-perfect life for Evelyn a thought that made her want to cry.

This summer was the worst it had ever been. Evelyn had

walked hand and hand with her husband Levi into the high-class house parties of the Hampton's elite, although her marriage was all but over. It had been at her urging that they acted as if things were still wonderful at home. Evelyn had also smiled, chuckled and told several people that her daughter was away in Europe studying anthropology, although her only child was tucked away from the probing eyes in drug rehab four hours away from the Hamptons. The best lie of all, however; was how Evelyn had played the role of a happy-go-lucky, faithful wife, although she had been plotting for months on how to get even with her husband by finding her own love affair. Evelyn had to admit, this time she felt more powerful than she ever had during her entire marriage. Yes, it was a crazy time at the Epstein home.

Evelyn didn't know how much more of a horse and pony show she could put on for all of her superficial, "happily married" friends. She was dying slowly inside. The fake smiles and all of the lies were wearing on her. She had literally watched her perfect life fade into obscurity. She was in a loveless marriage; her only child was a drug addict; and, now she had found out how her husband had been keeping them afloat financially all of these years since his family had shut him out of his late father's wealth. Things were spiraling downward fast. Evelyn had always thought of herself as being in full control of it all. Not now. The reality of just how little control she had was never more evident than now.

Evelyn closed her eyes when she heard Levi approaching from behind. She smelled his signature, Ralph Lauren Safari cologne before he even made it to where she stood. She flinched as Levi placed one hand on her shoulder and pecked her on her cheek. More like a brother would perfunctorily kiss his sister. "How are you?" he asked dryly. Evelyn cracked a halfhearted smile, her back going rigid and her shoulders stiffening under his touch. It was all she could do to keep her composure, to keep from punching, slapping, and spitting on him. She couldn't find one ounce of love left for her husband. Their once undying love had withered into contempt, resentments, and regrets. She was sure Levi could tell from her body language that she wasn't up for any small talk from him.

"You're up early," Levi commented, flashing a perfectly veneered fake smile. Levi wasn't going to let Evelyn kill his refreshed spirit with her normal sour mood. He never looked Evelyn in the eyes anymore. She knew it was because of his guilt for his latest conquest. "I guess you have your day planned already…" he continued the small talk with no response from Evelyn. He set something down next to him and by Evelyn's side. That got her attention right away. She looked down and peered at Levi's suitcase. She rolled her eyes and bit into her bottom lip. She could feel the heat rising from her chest, and her hands involuntarily curled into fists. Levi noticed his wife's body language. He wore an expression that said not again. The manufactured drama was getting old fast.

"I won't be gone long. I promise. I'll be back in time for Diane's annual all-white affair. I know how much that means to you," Levi explained, dryly garnering no response in his wife's body language. He knew that keeping up appearances for her friends was more important to Evelyn than anything he could ever do to make her happy again. Evelyn turned towards Levi abruptly, causing him to take a step back. She moved in like a lion towards its prey, her eyes in evil slits.

"Did you forget your daughter is graduating from the rehabilitation center today?" Evelyn asked, her voice low, almost a growl. She eyed him evilly, her nostrils moving in and out. She had one shaky finger jutted accusingly towards Levi, and her other hand balled so tightly her nails dug moon-shaped craters into her palms. She was tired of playing second fiddle in Levi's life. But, if he was going to treat her like she didn't exist…fine, but now their only child.

"I didn't forget. I told you I have a very important business meeting," he replied, annoyed. "I left her a gift on the table inside. There's a note there and a little something to make up for my absence," Levi finished flatly without looking his wife in the eyes. He immediately signaled for his driver to grab his bags. In his assessment, there was nothing else to talk about. Levi knew how their confrontations would end up. He had long since grown tired of Evelyn's constant guilt trips and self-pity parties. She had definitely become a shell of her former vibrant, outgoing, attention-commanding self. She was far from the woman he'd married.

"So that's it? You throw money at her again? A goddamn note Levi?! Is that all you can offer her?! You think a note can make up for your absence?!" Are we back to our same antics again? Your family comes second to the new whore!" Evelyn barked at her husband's back. "It was your money that got her where she is in the first place!" Levi gave her a look that sent a chill down her spine before he continued on.

"Levi! I am talking to you!" Evelyn called out again. He ignored her and rushed down the front steps. Before she could say another word, Levi climbed into the back of his Mercedes May Bach and slammed the door. Evelyn rocked on her heels as she watched the car ease down the long pathway towards the road. That was it. Just like that, Levi was gone again.

Evelyn had been through the same thing so many times she had come to expect it. She had recognized all of the signs that Levi was having yet another affair. It had been a month since she'd gotten the photographs from the private investigator that had confirmed her suspicions. This time Levi had crossed the line; he'd gotten disrespectful and disgusting with his philandering. When Evelyn had reviewed the photos of Levi and his new mistress, she'd thrown up the entire contents of her stomach. The same gut sickening feeling had come over her again, but this time was different…more personal.

Evelyn could feel her heart throbbing against her chest bone now just thinking about it. She guessed this was what a broken heart felt like. It wasn't a new feeling, and she didn't know why it always felt like a fresh wound. Evelyn silently chastised herself for being so emotional all of the time. It had been twenty-two years since she'd met and married who she thought was the man of her dreams and he'd been unfaithful at least ten or more of those years. She closed her eyes to stifle the angry tears threatening to fall. Instead, she headed into the house to make a phone call. "Two can play the game this time around Levi Epstein," she mumbled as she stormed through the house. There would be no more victim roll for Evelyn. No. She planned to be victorious this time around.

****

Evelyn had just stepped off the runway at New York's Fashion week when she'd first met Levi in 1989. Evelyn's perfect ivory skin went flush with red when Levi approached her at the after-show reception. Everyone who was anyone in New York City knew who Levi Epstein was—the gorgeous and very wealthy son of Ari Epstein, New York's most wealthy real estate tycoon. It was a well-known fact that Levi Epstein could have any woman in the world he wanted. Not only was he strikingly attractive, he was rich and single, and the opportunities that came his way were abundant. He was thirty-five and number one on the most eligible bachelor list; a fact that was not lost on Evelyn when Levi approached her flashing his perfect smile and displaying the charm of a storybook prince. He immediately grabbed her hand and planted his perfect lips on the top of it. It was something like electricity that had coursed through Evelyn's body, but she had done a fabulous job of keeping her composure.

Standing together, they looked like the perfect Hollywood couple. Evelyn's statuesque six-foot frame was adorned with a beautiful, teal, Donna Karan dress that dipped low in the back exposing her firm, muscular frame. The dress had fit her svelte body like it had been sewn on. Perfectly coifed, dark brown, ringlets of hair danced around her face and picked up the chestnut in her eyes.

"You were stunning in the show," Levi had said to her. His smile was a lady-killer. Evelyn had felt a whoosh of breath leave her lungs in response to his smooth baritone. Although she looked like a grown woman, Evelyn was only nineteen years old and hadn't had much time to date. Levi's beautiful grey eyes and his neatly trimmed jet-black hair had overwhelmed her. He reminded Evelyn of a younger Brad Pitt. Looking at him made her pulse quicken, so she lowered her eyes, stared down into her drink, and smiled girlishly.

"You probably say that to all of the models," Evelyn murmured, still averting direct eye contact. Levi had placed his finger under her chin and urged her to look at him. Evelyn reluctantly locked eyes with him, and when he smiled, she swore she could feel her heart-melting. Standing in his presence, Evelyn felt like they were the only two people in the large, crowded ballroom. They'd spent the entire reception laughing and talking about everything from runway fashions to politics. Levi had asked Evelyn if he could call her sometime and maybe take her out. She'd told him that she was leaving for Milan the next day and would be gone for two months. Levi had told her that was all the more reason he wanted to get to know her— she was a woman with her own life. He'd asked if she would leave her contact information so that he could call her sometime. She scribbled her information down on a silver trimmed napkin. Levi pushed it into his lapel pocket. "Right next to my heart," he'd said, tapping the place where he had put her number. That made Evelyn blush all over again. She was smitten.

After her third day in Milan, Evelyn returned to her hotel one night to find the entire room filled with beautiful long stem pink, red, and white roses. She was flabbergasted when she'd read the card, "You are as pretty as a newly blossomed rose. I came to Milan just to see you. Please call. Levi Epstein."

Evelyn had flopped down on her bed, weak with joy. The other two lanky beauties she had been rooming with snickered and made love faces and googly eyes at her. "Call him! Call him," They had twirled around her, urging her to call Levi right away, but Evelyn opted to wait until the next day. She didn't want him to think she was that easy to win over. When she'd finally called, Levi officially asked her out on a date. They went on their first date, and it had been magical—a gondola ride, dinner at a quaint Italian eatery, and a romantic walk through the city at night. Evelyn was overwhelmed with feelings she'd never experienced in her life. It had to be love.

Levi had wanted to know all about her life. He'd been the first man to ever care about the little things that mattered to her, like her childhood and how she'd become a high fashion model at such a young age. They spent another night talking into the wee hours of the morning. It was like they had been made for each other from the start. Evelyn had never experienced anything like what she had that night. No one had ever shown her the kind of interest that Levi had shown her. Levi felt the same as well. He had always had women swooning over him, but none had ever held his interest as long as Evelyn had. It was like a fateful love that was meant to be from the start.

Levi stayed in Milan for a week wining and dining Evelyn after her fashion photoshoots and shows. He wanted to make sure that she knew that he wanted her; that he was interested in her; and that, he intended on making this a regular occurrence. He'd showered her with beautiful premier designer gifts. Levi had spared no expense. He felt like it was the least he could do for this beauty he had found. Before he left Milan, Levi asked Evelyn to call him when she returned to New York. She had initially acted as if she had had to "think about it," but Evelyn knew the real truth about how she was feeling inside. She could hardly sit still for her entire flight from Milan to New York City. Evelyn had called as soon as her plane landed at JFK Airport. Her hands had trembled as she had dialed his number from a cold payphone right inside of the airport. Evelyn was relieved when he'd answered. She literally melted inside once she was able to speak to the man; she knew she was falling in love with. Levi was all she could think of for the time she remained in Milan without him. She had crazy feelings of longing. So much so that the other girls had teased her incessantly until their job in Milan was done.

Evelyn and Levi met the day after her return to New York, and they had officially begun dating. Levi had given her a single flower he'd picked from Central Park and said, "would you be mine?" They had shared a hearty laugh at Levi's antics, but Evelyn had surely accepted the little wilting flower and his invitation to date him.

Levi made Evelyn feel like she was the only woman in the world every single day. There was never a dull moment with him. Not only did he shower her with gifts, but he'd taken her to all of New York's most exclusive invite-only social events and acted as if he was so proud to have her on his arm. Levi was such a gentleman. He was extremely, loving, and he paid attention to every detail of their relationship. People always commented on what a beautiful couple they made. After a year of dating, Levi finally proposed. When he'd presented Evelyn with his great grandmother's sapphire and diamond engagement ring, Evelyn almost wet herself. She jumped into his arms screaming, "yes! yes! yes!" Levi's parents weren't happy with his choice. They would have preferred a good, clean, Jewish girl for their youngest son. Evelyn had grown up Catholic. She was certainly no virgin if she was a model; Levi's mother had complained. Evelyn also didn't have parents, which alarmed the Epsteins. "What is a girl without a mother?! No mother, no religion, what else Levi!" Levi's mother had screamed in her usual theatrical performance manner. Levi had heard his mother's "dream girl" for him so many times that he went out and found the complete opposite.

Evelyn so head over heels in love quickly agreed to go through the process of converting to Judaism. Levi's parents; defeated by Evelyn and Levi's love; finally settled. Evelyn and Levi were married in a traditional Jewish ceremony. The wedding took place on a white sand beach adjacent to Ari Epstein's $40 million-dollar estate in the Caribbean island of Turks and Caicos. Four hundred guests attended the lavish wedding; of which, only twenty-five were Evelyn's friends—people she'd befriended while modeling. The remainder of the guests she'd never even met. At the time, Evelyn didn't dare complain. She felt like she was living a dream; far from what she could have ever envisioned for herself. As an orphan who'd grown up poor, Evelyn never dreamed she'd become a world-renowned model, but more importantly, that she'd be married to one of the most coveted men in the United States. On all accounts, Evelyn thought she'd walked into heaven. It didn't take long for her to realize she'd been sadly mistaken. Life with Levi had changed so drastically, sometimes Evelyn couldn't believe he was the same man she'd met back then.

"Mrs. Epstein your car is out front," Carolynn announced snapping Evelyn out of her reverie. Evelyn hadn't even realized she'd been staring into space. She quickly dabbed at her eyes and turned towards Carolynn. Carolynn smiled at her, realizing she had interrupted Evelyn's thoughts.

"I want everything to be perfect for Arianna when she gets here. Please make sure the caterers are on time and the tent...the decorations have to be perfect. Her favorite color is blue. The cake is supposed to be delivered in two hours. The guests should arrive...I just..." Evelyn rambled; an edge of nerves apparent in her words. Carolynn put her hand up and let a warm smile spread across her face. She knew her boss was nervous.

"Mrs. E, I will have everything in order. I know how important this day is to you and to Ari," Carolynn comforted, her warm smile easing the tension in the air. Evelyn exhaled and thanked Carolynn. She trusted Carolynn who'd worked for the family since Arianna was born. Only, Evelyn, Levi, and Carolynn knew the truth about the purpose of the big party. Carolynn knew all of the family's secrets. She had become a part of their family; thus, she knew every detail of their lives. She followed Evelyn around the huge master suite making sure Evelyn didn't forget anything. Carolynn gave the room a once over. Everything seemed to be all right.

Evelyn grabbed her Hermes Birkin and looked at herself one last time in the long Victorian-style mirror that took up almost an entire wall in the master suite. She was still a knockout, even at forty-one years old. Admittedly, she had a little help from one of the top plastic surgeons in New York, a nip here and a tuck there, but her natural beauty still came through. Her face showed only a few crow's feet at the corners of her eyes, nothing a little Restylane couldn't cure she thought. She'd just gotten rid of her laugh lines a week prior, and she'd gotten her lips filled in while she was at it. Evelyn had opted to use collagen fillers instead of Botox-like most of her friends. Carolynn smiled as she watched her boss go over her outfit again and again. It was a habit Evelyn hadn't broken in all these years. Carolynn knew Evelyn's next move before she even did it. Just as anticipated, Evelyn ran her hands over the flat part of her stomach and turned sideways to make sure her Spanx were doing their job. It was flat as a board. Perfect.

She wore a pair of white, wide-legged crepe Versace sailor pants that complimented her long, still model-like slim legs. Carolyn assisted Evelyn as she shrugged into a short, navy Diane Von Furstenberg blazer to complete her look. Evelyn adjusted her newly lifted D cup breasts and examined her neck and jaw lines to make sure her tanning bed hadn't left any streaks. She smiled at herself and then back at Carolynn.

"Not so bad for the mother of an eighteen-year-old, huh Carolynn?" Evelyn posed the question she really didn't want the answer to.

"Beautiful," Carolynn praised on queue. They'd had this same routine for the longest.

Evelyn chuckled. She knew she was the quintessential kept woman. Through it all, she had managed to keep herself in tiptop shape, and with the assistance of her plastic surgeon, she still got mistaken for a woman in her thirties. As she headed out of the house towards her waiting ride, her cell phone buzzed in her bag. Evelyn fished around and retrieved it. Instinctively a smile spread across her face. "Hello lover," she cooed into the mobile device as she slid into the back of the Bentley that awaited her. Evelyn closed her eyes; maybe the day wouldn't be as bad as she'd thought it would be. Especially if she could slip away after she did her motherly duty.

Chapter Two
Family First

People rushed around her, but that didn't distract Evelyn at all. She kept her head up high as she sat on one of the hard-wooden seats inside the auditorium of the Passages Rehabilitation Center. Her palms were sweaty, and she couldn't keep her legs from rocking back and forth. Evelyn was clearly out of her element, but she knew she had to be there regardless. She kept telling herself, "it is my duty."

Evelyn looked around at some of the parents there, just like her, most seemed to be well off. Evelyn tried not to stare too long, but she couldn't help it. She felt a pang of jealousy looking at some of the couples holding hands and being supportive of each other. Seemingly happy families made her stomach churn. She wished that were her life again. Damn you, Levi.

Evelyn shook her head to clear it and tried to focus on why she was there—for her child. Her only child. And it had cost them $100,000 to get Arianna the treatment she needed.

It was an expense neither Evelyn nor Levi could argue wasn't necessary. Private drug rehabilitation was expensive, but in Evelyn's assessment, there was no amount of money that could keep her from trying to save her daughter or save face with her friends was more like it. There was no way Evelyn could stand for any of her socialite friends to find out Arianna was addicted to drugs and had been living like a virtual vagabond. The thought of anyone finding out made a cold chill shoot down Evelyn's spine. She hunched her shoulders in an attempt to relax, but the thoughts still hovered.

Evelyn remembered clearly how devastated she was when she found out their princess was addicted to methamphetamine. It was Carolynn who'd nervously told Evelyn about Arianna's addiction. Evelyn also thought back to how Levi had screamed at her and told her it was all her fault that his daughter was an embarrassment to the Epstein name. He had told Evelyn it was Evelyn's "trashy" DNA and family lineage that had caused their daughter to be such a disappointment. It hadn't been the first time Levi had used Evelyn's upbringing against her during an argument.

"Mother," Evelyn heard the familiar voice from behind her. She popped up out of her seat and cleared away the thoughts that had been crowding her mind. Evelyn took in an eyeful of her only child. She tilted her head and clasped her hand over her mouth.

Tears welled up in her eyes immediately when she went to grab for her daughter.

"Oh, sweetheart…you look amazing. This time away has done wonders. I am so proud of you," Evelyn cried, grabbing her daughter in a tight embrace. Evelyn felt a warm feeling of relief wash over her. Arianna finally presented like something Evelyn could be proud of. Evelyn squeezed Arianna again. "Thank God," she whispered. Evelyn was really thanking God for bringing her daughter back from the brink of death. What would her friends have thought if Arianna had gave way to a drug addiction? Evelyn would've suffered the worst embarrassment of her life. Evelyn shook off those worse case scenarios and tried to relish in the moment.

It was a miracle that Arianna was even alive. The night Evelyn and Levi had signed Arianna into the rehabilitation center involuntarily, Arianna had looked like death warmed over. Her skin had been ghostly pale, and dark rings rimmed the bottoms of her eyes. Arianna's dark hair had been matted in clumps around her scalp, and her body was gaunt, almost skeletal. She smelled like she hadn't had a bath in weeks and her clothes, although expensive, were filthy. Arianna had been out on a binge for three weeks while Evelyn and Levi worried sick and had people out scouring the entire city for her. It had been the first time they'd come together for anything in years. Levi had even hugged

Evelyn a few of the nights they'd both sat up worrying about their daughter. Arianna had kicked and screamed when she'd first arrived at the center. She cursed at her parents and told her mother she hated her. She'd screamed and begged Levi not to let Evelyn sign her into the center. Arianna blamed Evelyn for everything. Evelyn was an emotional wreck that night. She also blamed herself for it all, although she knew it wasn't entirely her fault. Levi had remained cool as a cucumber, as usual. "Daddy loves you. Daddy loves you," Levi had repeated to his daughter over and over again. He never once defended Evelyn and told his daughter she needed the help. It was something Evelyn filed in her mental Rolodex. The hurt she'd felt was almost tangible.

All of that was the past Evelyn told herself now. Just like all of the other hurts she'd suffered at the hands of her daughter and husband, Evelyn swallowed them like hard marbles. Seeing Arianna now—cheeks rosy, body filled out in all of the right places, hair shiny and straight, made Evelyn warm inside. Arianna had taken the best of Evelyn and Levi's features. She stood almost six feet tall and was built like a runway model. She had long slender legs, a small waist, and small breasts. Arianna had exquisite, thick, jet-black hair and slate grey eyes. She had inherited Evelyn's high cheekbones and perfect nose, and with Levi's prominent chin, her face was striking. From the time she was a small child, Arianna had turned heads everywhere she went. She was more of a showstopper than both of her parents to say the least.

Evelyn finally relinquished her grasp on Arianna and gave her a good once over. Evelyn smiled wide; she thought her daughter looked perfect. Arianna was dressed conservatively in a maroon Donna Karan sheath dress that Carolynn had picked out; a pair of kitten-heeled Jimmy Choo's and a simple cardigan to top off her look. Arianna finally looked like an eighteen-year-old wealthy J.A.P (Jewish American Princess) should. Evelyn was satisfied, but she still couldn't say she was ever proud to say that Arianna was her daughter. It had always been a struggle being a mother to Arianna. Evelyn squeezed Arianna and grabbed for Arianna's hand, hoping to get a return show of affection. But Arianna impolitely let her arms hang limp at her side. Evelyn knew right away that her daughter was in rare form. It was the norm for Arianna to treat Evelyn like she had no regard for her at all.

"Where's dad?" Arianna asked petulantly. Evelyn released her daughter's hand quickly. She looked at Arianna seriously. She wanted to scream in Arianna's face and say I am here for you! Isn't that enough! He was never there for you like I have been! But Evelyn kept her thoughts to herself; kept smiling and kept doing what she did best—pretending.

"Oh, Ari darling, this is your day. Don't worry about

the small things. You look so good…so healthy now," Evelyn replied sympathetically. She cracked a phony smile and hugged her daughter again, hoping they could move off the subject of Levi. "You are simply stunning Ari, I can't say that enough," Evelyn followed up, flashing her plastic smile again. Nothing seemed to faze Arianna.

"I guess you would say I look good now since you haven't seen me in six months. All you have to compare it to is the way I looked when you forced me into this hell hole," Arianna replied sharply, as she squirmed out of her mother's stifling embrace. Evelyn felt like someone had slapped her across the face. She inhaled. It was taking all she had to keep it together now.

Evelyn ignored the comment. She already felt awful enough about not visiting, but she'd figured that Arianna needed time away without the influence of her parents. Evelyn had been afraid that if she'd visited, Arianna would ask her questions about her father. Evelyn had always tried to shelter Arianna from the reality that her father was a philandering whore. Evelyn's sugar-coating Levi's indiscretions only made Arianna see Evelyn as the bad guy and Levi as the hero in their lives. The past six months had been no different. Levi cheated, and Evelyn covered up. She hid his ways from Arianna; their friends; his parents… everyone. It became like a fulltime job for Evelyn. Faking, like her life, was still picture perfect. This time was slightly different. Now as Arianna shot accusing eyes at her, Evelyn guiltily thought about her own preoccupation while her daughter was gone and wanted to veer away from the topic of why she didn't visit.

"So are you ready to go home? You must be excited to get back to life. There are so many good things waiting for you. Whatever you want, you can have," Evelyn asked, changing the subject while fidgeting with her newly purchased monstrous twelve-carat canary diamond ring. It was one of many things she'd purchased on spite after finding out the identity of Levi's most recent mistress.

"Yeah going home…I can hardly wait to get back to that life. I'll see you after the ceremony," Arianna droned gruffly, stomping away from her mother. Evelyn looked around to see if anyone had noticed the strained interaction between them. She smiled weakly at a couple that had been watching. Evelyn's cheeks flamed over when she noticed them. She wondered how much of the conversation they had overheard. "These children. We have to love them," Evelyn chortled, averting her eyes away from the gawking pair. She turned her face away and dabbed at the tears threatening to drop from her eyes. Even her baby girl hated her. Evelyn couldn't win for trying. Nothing was ever good enough for Arianna and Levi. Years later, she still couldn't please them.

****

The night Arianna was born Levi had missed the entire birth—
from labor to the minute Arianna took her first breath. Evelyn
had spent sixteen hours in labor at Lenox Hill Hospital, and Levi
never showed up for a minute of it. Both of Levi's parents had
come rushing into Evelyn's private birthing room in a huff when
they'd gotten the news that their newest member was about to
arrive. But neither of them could explain why their son hadn't
been around when Evelyn tried to reach him. Levi's parents
had long since stopped making excuses for Levi because they
knew Evelyn wasn't buying it anymore. Evelyn felt that their
presence at the birth was only because they secretly hoped she
would provide them with a grandson to carry on the Epstein
name. Evelyn had known for months she was carrying a baby
girl, but she never told Levi or his parents. She knew how Jews
really felt about having first-born girls. She also knew they only
tolerated her as it was. Evelyn hadn't felt that alone in a room
full of people since her days living in an orphanage. Nurses,
Levi's parents, doctors, all circled around her, providing for her
every need. But no one could soothe the ache of loneliness she
felt for Levi.

After a horrendous labor, Evelyn had given birth to a
perfect little girl through cesarean section. She'd made sure

she got her tummy tucked at the same time. She wouldn't have wanted to disappoint Levi by not keeping herself up. Evelyn had already suspected that Levi was stepping out with other women behind her back.

The baby girl was a perfect, pink-faced, screaming bundle of joy. She had Levi's grey eyes and prominent chin, with Evelyn's long limbs and button nose. "Let's call her Ari... after her grandfather," Levi's mother had said after she laid eyes on her granddaughter. Ari Epstein, Levi's father agreed and who was Evelyn to argue with such a powerful patriarch. Whatever the Epsteins wanted, the Epsteins got. Evelyn had learned that the hard way. The naming of her first child would be no different. Evelyn, too physically and mentally exhausted to protest, compromised with the Epstein's and they all agreed to call the baby, Arianna Bethany Epstein. Or baby Ari for short. Evelyn thought it was a fair compromise given the fact that she had always wanted to name her first daughter Beth Ann, after a mother she had never known. She never told the Epsteins of her desires; instead, she came up with a name she thought she could live with.

When Levi finally showed up at the hospital to see his new baby, he smelled of a woman's perfume and looked like he'd been partying for days. He leaned in to give Evelyn an obligatory kiss, and she had turned her face away. It was all she could do to keep from making a scene in front of Levi's parents and to hide the hot tears that were threatening to spring from her eyes. Evelyn had tried to hold onto her anger and bitterness that first night Levi came to her bedside, but, after witnessing Levi hold his daughter with such care and sensitivity and watching him seemingly fall in love with his daughter, Evelyn had been overwhelmed with that old, gushy, head-over-heels feeling for Levi once again. It was like when they were in Milan, falling in love all over again. Evelyn had told herself that night in the hospital that for her child and the sake of her family, she would do anything it took to make them happy. It was a promise she would come to suffer to keep.

Things were great for a while after Arianna's birth. Evelyn felt like she'd finally gotten her husband back. In the beginning, Levi was a doting father and a caring husband. He showered Evelyn with gift after expensive gift. He'd told her the gifts were to thank her for giving him his greatest gift of all. He spent hours holding baby Ari, talking, and singing to her. So much so, Evelyn had shamefully grown a little jealous of how much attention Levi showered on the baby. But once again, Evelyn put her feelings aside and tried to make the best of the situation. Evelyn saw herself as just mother and wife. There was no more individual Evelyn. The things she wanted, needed and liked came secondary in her life. Evelyn spent every waking minute pleasing her daughter and her husband. She'd lost herself in meeting the needs of Levi and Arianna. But it was with the help of the hired hands of course. At some point, Evelyn grew to resent her life. Each day, she would perfunctorily put on a happy face.

As Arianna grew older, Evelyn and Levi gave her anything she asked for…materially anyway. From birth, Arianna was a trust fund baby. She was worth more than some celebrities five times her age, and she hadn't even turned a year old. Papa Epstein, which is what Levi's father asked to be called, had made sure his granddaughter would never have to lift a finger in her life. Evelyn felt a sense of security knowing that unlike herself as a child, her daughter would never want for anything.

There were extravagant nurseries built for baby Ari in every home Levi owned, even in his two New York City penthouses. Arianna was royalty in the eyes of the entire Epstein family. She had been given dance lessons from the age of two. She had a private acting coach as soon as she turned five. Papa Ari purchased a thoroughbred riding horse for Arianna's tenth birthday and equestrian lessons to match. She'd had huge, extravagant birthday parties every year with a guest list of A-list celebrity children. For her Bat Mitzvah, they'd flown in dresses from Paris, Milan, and London. Once a year Evelyn and Levi would take Arianna on vacation to parts of the world she couldn't even pronounce. Private schools were the only kind ever considered for Arianna. She'd been provided an allowance of $1,000 per week from the time she was thirteen years old. Even after the huge Bat Mitzvah, Arianna's sweet sixteen was thrown on a yacht and cost more than some celebrity weddings. But, as she got older, Arianna realized that nothing her parents gave her could replace spending time with them every day or having at least one sit down dinner with them like she'd seen done in families on television. Carolynn was the person who showed up for school meetings, plays, and trips. Levi and Evelyn hardly knew anything concrete about their daughter's wants and needs. Evelyn was too busy keeping tabs on Levi to notice.

After a while, nothing Levi and Evelyn gave Arianna seemed like enough. They poured money into any activity she picked up—gymnastics, soccer, synchronized swimming, lacrosse, equestrian, golf, polo, and, tennis. Arianna would grow bored and quit. She had grown to be spoiled and angry. By the time she was seventeen, Arianna was deep into the New York party and drug scene. She fashioned herself as one of New York City's brat pack socialites. Late night party scenes became her daily life. She'd grown up and become best friends with former child stars, daughters of hotel magnates and children of rock stars. Unflattering paparazzi pictures of Arianna had shown up at least two dozen times in People and Us magazines.

When confronted, Arianna would scream and throw tantrums. Evelyn had admittedly dropped the ball when it came to paying her daughter the attention she was craving. But she blamed Levi for it all, and he blamed her just the same.

****

Evelyn and Arianna's ride from the rehabilitation center was tensely silent. It was as if a joyous occasion had not just happened. Arianna was brooding the entire ride, and Evelyn was trying to please as usual. The pomp and circumstance of Arianna's rehab graduation faded quicker than an eclipse of the sun. Afterward, Evelyn had tried to make small talk, about the weather, Arianna's clothes, her new cell phone. When that didn't work, Evelyn tried to tell Arianna how proud she was of her accomplishments—getting clean and sober in six months. Evelyn had told Arianna that she imagined it hadn't been easy. Arianna ignored her mother, for the most part, dropping a vicious insult in response here and there. It wasn't lost on either of them how many times Evelyn's cell phone had buzzed and interrupted their tense exchange. Arianna had even raised an eyebrow to her mother and said, "Why don't you stop pretending to be interested in speaking to me and just answer your phone?" Evelyn's cheeks had flamed over at her daughter's comment. "No one is more important that you Ari," Evelyn had replied.

It didn't make a difference. She was clearly not going to make Arianna happy.

Finally, too exasperated to continue practically begging her daughter to talk to her, Evelyn gave up. Arianna rudely put her iPod earphones in and turned the volume up so loud Evelyn could hear every curse word in the lyrics of the rock music she listened to. Arianna also took to texting incessantly on her cell phone, one of the luxuries she had missed while locked up in that place. Defeated, Evelyn resorted to watching the passing scenery outside of the Bentley's darkly tinted windows. Evelyn secretly wished she were someplace else. She could think of a million things she would've rather be doing than taking her daughter's verbal abuse. Evelyn's mind drifted to things she found pleasurable. Of course, she thought about Max, her new friend. The thoughts seemed to ease the pain of the long ride. Evelyn found herself growing a little flush with some of the thoughts Max conjured in her mind.

When the car pulled up to the gate leading up to the house, Arianna yanked her earphones out of her ears and bolted upright in her seat. "I'm not going to the summer house, I'm going to the city…the penthouse," she announced brusquely. Evelyn's eyebrows shot up, and her pulse sped up. Arianna had been practically living alone at their Upper East Side penthouse when she'd disappeared and ultimately gotten herself in trouble.

Evelyn didn't think it was a good idea for her to go back into that environment so soon. Evelyn wanted Carolynn to keep an eye on Arianna. Of course, Evelyn didn't have time herself for babysitting a teenager right now. That's what they'd paid Carolynn to do all of these years.

"Ari, please," Evelyn said as calmly as she could given the circumstances. "You need to be around us…your loved ones. We all missed you so much. Carolynn is looking forward to seeing you. I want to catch up. You can go to the penthouse another day," Evelyn tried to reason, touching her daughter's leg gently. Arianna tilted her head and looked at her mother through squinted eyes. The look sent a chill down Evelyn's back.

"Please mother. Don't start this bullshit. Concerned mother doesn't fit you well. You don't want to catch up or spend quality time with me…you never have and never will," Arianna hissed, pushing Evelyn's hand off of her knee roughly. Evelyn snatched her hand back as if a venomous snake had bitten her. She pinched the bridge of her nose, trying to quell the throbbing that had suddenly started between her eyes. It was starting again, already—the hate/hate relationship she had with her only child. Evelyn often blamed herself for not bonding with Arianna as a baby. She let out a long breath that seemed to zap all of her energy. Everything seemed to stand still.

"I don't want to be here if my father is not here. I'm

over the Hamptons and all of your fake friends. I'm sure you have some kind of party planned for me in there, but I'm not coming. I refuse to be like you mother…a fucking fake, hiding behind money, Botox, and designer clothes… living a big lie. Now either you let me go where I want to go, or you get even more embarrassed when I go in there and tell everyone what a wonderful time, I had in drug rehab," Arianna spat viciously. Evelyn coughed or more like gagged. She felt like her daughter had gut-punched her. She placed her hand on her chest, shocked by her daughter's outburst. She looked over at her only child, and she swore she could see red flames flickering in Arianna's eyes. Pure hatred clouded the girls face. Evelyn's jaw rocked feverishly, and her pulse pounded. Suddenly everything was swirling around her. She cleared her throat like she'd done so many times when preparing to speak to Levi, thinking, Arianna had grown to be just like her father. Evelyn knew she couldn't let Arianna ruin what she had spent years building—the lie that was their life.

"Arianna, I have tried and tried. What more do you want me to do? It is not my fault that your father is not here. I asked him to be here, and he chose to attend a business meeting…" Evelyn started, steeling herself for more cruelty from Arianna. Arianna's face lit blood red, her eyebrows folded into a scowl.

"No! Shut up!" Arianna screamed. "You probably

ran him off like you always do. I don't know how he stayed married to you after all of these years with all of your nagging and complaining. Matter of fact, I do know. He stayed with you because of me! It's my fault that my poor father has to endure life with a bitch like you!" Arianna continued with her vituperative tirade. She yanked on the door handle, as the car had started moving through the open gate up the pathway to the house. The driver slammed on the breaks in response. Evelyn's body jerked forward then back, and her head slammed into the headrest. Her heart began pounding even harder, and her head throbbed.

"Oh, my God! Arianna!" Evelyn screamed, wincing, and holding the back of her head. The car had screeched to a halt, and Arianna scrambled out of the door. There was nothing Evelyn could do now.

"Ari! Wait!" Evelyn hung her head out of the door and screamed. It was too late. Visibly shaken, Evelyn decided against running after her daughter. There was, but so much she could take. She knew that Arianna was serious when she said she would tell everyone she was not in Europe; but in a rehab. Someplace deep inside, what all of her friends thought was more important than forcing her daughter to enjoy the lavish party she had prepared.

"Everything alright, Mrs. E?" their driver asked. Evelyn was terribly embarrassed and equally as flustered. "You want me to go after her?" he asked, peering at Evelyn through the rearview mirror.

"I'm fine. She's a teenager," Evelyn replied, trying to seem lighthearted about the incident, but not able to control her voice shaking. "Take me up to the house and come back for her. Take her wherever she wants to go. If she wants to go to the city, let her go to the city," Evelyn croaked out instructions to the driver, her voice finally shedding the false cheeriness she tried on; instead, her words came out laced with pain and anger. It was better than Arianna blowing the whistle on Evelyn's lies.

Once in front of the house, Evelyn climbed from the car. She steeled herself for the questions and shocked looks she knew she'd face when she stepped inside of her home. Evelyn immediately began constructing more lies in her head. She had become so good at it now that it took her no time to think of what she'd tell her friends about Arianna's whereabouts. Evelyn exhaled a windstorm before she turned the doorknob to her home. It was the first time she had acknowledged that she was losing the battle on all fronts, but she'd made it up in her mind that it wouldn't be for long.